AMIR OF GUELPH

Amir of Guelph

ALBERT MARSOLAIS

Marsolais & Twigg Publishing

CONTENTS

A speculation for those who care about the future.

| 1 |

Chapter One

I needed to see Ranjit and he had practically moved into the senior's centre on Woolwich Street after the recent rash of harassments. Seniors had become the most despised segment of society, especially those of us who looked much younger than our nominal age because of ReGen treatments. The overly friendly guard at the screening booth smirked as I was scanned. "You're one of those, aren't you?" he said, intruding in my info space.

It is best not to react to blatant breaches of protocol, so I merely nodded and left immediately. Ranjit was waiting in the greeting area, twisting his magnificent upturned black moustache that made him look like a throwback to the Raj. He was rotund but fit, directed synaptic stimulation keeping him toned despite the eighteen hours a day he spends in his Divine Life virtual reality cradle.

That morning he left a thought in my implant and wanted some real with me, at my earliest convenience, please and thank you, dear old friend, so forth. Ranjit was very polite in that new way. It was a risk coming here since the centre was a frequent target but our careers in government many decades ago had intersected and I owed him muchly for providing the right introductions.

"Amir, so good to see you!" he blurted in his effusive manner. I offered a hand to shake, a bad old habit, I know. He more properly slipped his hands under his armpits and a took a step back, nodding and smiling.

"We need privacy. Come this way. I have a room," Ranjit said too loudly for my taste. We gracefully dodged our way down the crowded hall to the row of small rooms that could be rented by the hour. He briefly looked at the scanner and the door clicked open. Privacy had become a valuable service as people were forced to live closer together for security and economic reasons. The room was white and spare with a well-scarred laminate table and two chairs, and a shelf with a fading sign that: "No Sex Allowed", and in the corner, a bin for refuse streaming. I knew Ranjit had few credits left over after paying necessities and ReGen treatments, so I was curious that he had splurged so much for this room.

When we sat, he clasped his hands on the table, and in a terribly serious voice announced, "I have not seen Lei for more than a week." He closed is eyes momentarily to consult his Artificial Intelligence implant. "Eight days and nine hours, actually."

I waited for him to continue, but he just sat there looking like he had said enough already, and that I should clearly understand the significance. I had been expecting something more momentous since he had spent so much for the venue. "She didn't leave a thought?" I asked, trying to fathom the problem.

"No and I've sent thoughts to her every day. We were to have presented an important idea at the cybergenuity workshop together, and she didn't show. I had half the idea and she the other, so it was very embarrassing presenting half an idea like that." He stressed the word "very" and twisted his mouth and I imagined he must have been squirming in his cradle, cursing her.

"I assume you tried pinging...to see if her AI was on?" It was an obvious first step and I did not want to insult him, but the on/off switch was the first thing techs check.

He gave me that sour look when he believes I think he is an idiot. "Of course, I checked, and it isn't on. Could be switched off, or defective, or..." His voice halted when his mind must have seized on some of the more worrisome possibilities.

"Do you know where she lives in real?"

"Yes, in one of those pod homes on the old university lands. Don't know which one though. Never been there."

"You've met her in real...right?"

"No, just in Divine Life."

I was puzzled by his concern. People take breaks all the time. "Hmm, let me guess. You have a relationship with her in DL, don't you?"

"Amir...you mustn't tell anyone, but yes we've been lovers for a few years. That's why I'm so worried. She wouldn't leave without telling me."

I so wanted to make a smart remark or smack him, but instead decided to be the supportive friend he deserved. "Tell me about her, then."

Over the next twenty minutes he did, and it was not easy

keeping him on track, but I learned that Lei was on Re-Gen treatments but struggling to make the payments and was fond of combat roleplay games. Not much to go on. While I went over a few scenarios in my mind, he sat back in his chair waiting for me to come up with the perfect plan.

I finally decided that siting there musing and staring at each other would not be fruitful, so opted to begin at the beginning, as they say. "Let's go over and have a look. Get her pod number and I'll treat for a car."

There was a lineup of hire cars at the semi-circular entrance to the senior's centre. I thought for one and Ranjit entered the destination address. Most of us lived in small self-sorted communities of mutual need and walk where we want to go. Transport between communities was by minibus and hire cars. Our car quickly took us to an area at the university that had once been lecture halls, re-purposed for a world without on-site students. The university had discovered years ago that many enjoyed living there and hence they had built highly profitable housing that saved it from financial ruin.

"This must be it." I looked up at the massive white modular building which had been printed and assembled in less than a month. There were hundreds of units arrayed in rows and columns like a spreadsheet. The university advertised them as personal executive suites, but the rest of us called them pods. Ranjit shared thoughts with the main entrance sensor and the floor conveyor and lift promptly took us directly to her unit.

"I hope she's here," Ranjit said with a quiver in his voice. He could have done this himself, but he was so cerebral that having his body do something must have been terrifying. So,

I was happy to escort him, and fully expected a quick resolution and chuckle as a surprised girlfriend opened the door.

He sent a thought to the sensor at her door and audibly whispered, "It's me Ranjit." The pods are only about eight feet square and have all the basics to sustain life, plus two major features: they are cheap, and they are equipped with a Divine Life cradle hooked to the university's massive network. For DL addicts, it is heaven. There are even common areas and shops for necessities on every floor, so one never needs to leave.

"No answer. I'll try again," he mumbled.

"Try the admin AI too. Ask if she's been in."

"Admin won't tell me. Says I'm not on her whitelist," he said that with a look of disappointment blended with a hint of betrayal which I had seen many times when he faced one of life's minor setbacks.

"Then tell admin she's been missing for a week and her emergency contacts need to be notified."

"Done."

We waited for a few moments, then Ranjit shook his head and said, "Nothing."

There was another option, and I voiced it loudly, "I can hack the door!" Ranjit looked at me in shock. Everyone knew there was universal surveillance, and my utterance would have been picked up by one or another security AI and orders already were being prepared to zap my brain and pick me up for psycho-treatment. At least that was what people said would happen to rule-breakers like me. I had to chance it though. Lei was missing and her contacts not responding, and I knew Ranjit was going to implode if we did not find her soon.

For the record, my implant was not zapped, but the police did arrive a few minutes later. We explained the situation and as usual they were annoyingly kind and considerate and ordered the admin AI to override the door locks so they could enter. Turned out the pod looked well-lived in, but no Lei and no indication of where she might have gone.

We stood there perplexed. People seldom go missing these days. Implants were made mandatory a generation ago and you could not legally buy or sell anything without them, so it was hard to exist without it being recorded somewhere.

Ranjit took a deep breath and formally addressed the police. "I know it is an imposition, and I'm only a friend, and she's only been gone a week and her emergency contacts haven't responded—"

The smiling policewoman thankfully cut him off. "We are doing a scan now. If the implant is working, we'll find your friend."

They know where everyone is and what they are doing through the thought communications implant and imbedded AI. That alone pretty much eliminated crime and the need for prisons, since everyone committing any offense could be caught, evaluated, and immediately sent for psycho-treatment. That is how it is supposed to work, anyway.

"No result, and the occupant hasn't been registered as deceased," the policewoman said without inflection. "I guess we need to up this a level. A search team will be assigned. I need permission to access your implants for basic info." We both agreed and a minute later she asked, "Is Zhang Lei, a rider?"

I cringed hearing that derogatory term for seniors who were on life extending treatments. It implied "free-rider" and encapsulated how the rest saw us, as selfish people who used far more resources than we deserved. We saw it differently. The ReGen treatments are expensive and not covered by insurance, and as a result most of us have made considerable changes in our lifestyle to afford them. It was a choice, nothing more. Most have chosen to live big while they can. We to live long. Few get both. That is why it is galling to be so reviled. They could have done the same had they sacrificed a vacation or two when they were young. I halted my inner rant just in time to avoid saying something stupid.

"Can't you check? Why ask us?" It was Ranjit responding to the policewoman's question, and I could tell by the tone he was becoming testy, so I sent a thought shushing him.

"You must know we've had a few of your kind...umm...drained...for their blood, but the perpetrator hasn't been caught." She consulted her AI for background, and I instantly wished she had not been so forthright.

"Wasn't that tried years ago? I mean harvesting blood plasma from ReGen people?" I remembered dimly.

"Yes, and it didn't work, if I recall from my senior's crime course."

"No, it wouldn't, the treatments take years, and a large part is epigenetic and cleaning therapy that isn't transferable in plasma."

"Ignorance has never stopped idiots before," she nodded sagely.

Ranjit was becoming visibly agitated and I had to get him out of there, so I sent him a quick thought and said goodbye to the police officer. She transferred a document with logs and an action plan as we left.

Ranjit sat in the hire car with a scowl that aged him twenty years and once we got going grumbled, "That was a waste of time. The police weren't much help, were they?"

"It *was* well worth our time. We found out a lot, actually, and the police are doing their best, Ranjit." I could not let his pessimism stand. He does not cope well in real and I knew it. He shrugged, then remained gloomily silent the rest of the way back to the senior's centre.

As soon as we entered the greeting area, the woman at the desk waved him over. "You have a message," she said, then slid a piece of paper over the counter to him. He looked at it, not comprehending. No one sent paper messages anymore. I grabbed it and read aloud. It was from Zhang Lei and said she was well and to meet her at six-o-clock at the coordinates written on the paper.

Ranjit whooped, "She is well!" He laughed so forcefully everyone looked. My AI quickly found the location of the co-ordinates. It was on a First Nations reserve an hour away by car. I pulled Ranjit to a quieter corner, him protesting about being touched.

"Ranjit, listen. What is she doing at a First Nations reserve with her implant off?"

He grinned at me. "It matters not, she is well, and we must fetch her. Can you lend me the credits?"

A generation ago, the naturals and First Nations formed an alliance to resist implants and universal surveillance. For credit exchanges they used a dark banking system, and the government could do little because of treaties going back hundreds of years. The First Nations made most of their credits renting homes to the naturals who wanted nothing to do with our system. It was never clear where the naturals made their credits, but most assumed it was illegal.

"Umm…alright we can go look, but this doesn't smell right to me." My mind was churning with possibilities of what could go wrong.

On the way, Ranjit was bubbling with happiness and I had to turn up the white noise in my implant lest my blood pressure rise to the forbidden zone. The location turned out to be a run-down house just inside the reserve. That made me extremely nervous since we legally should not be there, and our laws may not protect us if we got in any trouble.

I knocked on the door and heard a welcoming feminine voice respond, "Come in. It's open." Ranjit winked at me then opened the door. Inside, the living room was filled with junk plastic and corroded metal furniture, and in the doorway to the kitchen stood an incredibly old Asian man holding an equally old pistol, pointed at us.

"It is so nice to finally meet you, my beloved Ranjit," he said in a seductive voice produced by the speaker at his throat.

Ranjit stood there looking like he was rapidly sliding into shock. He could only get out one word: "Lei?"

"Indeed, it is me my darling. Thank you for bringing him. I desperately need his blood."

| 2 |

Chapter Two

It had been almost three months since the fiasco with Zhang Lei and I had not seen nor heard from Ranjit till he contacted me earlier today and requested a meeting. I was still annoyed with him, but he said he would make it worth my while financially. I was dubious but had nothing better to do, so we met in the park behind the senior's centre. It was awkward at first, but time had taken the edge off the bad memory and it was good to see him looking the same in his voluminous robes and distinctive moustache. After the awkward pleasantries, Ranjit transferred an investment brochure to me.

He started talking before I had a chance to read. "It's the perfect investment, Amir. Pays one percent a month on capital invested. The banks don't give anything near that, and the kicker is that the rate goes up as people die, and the last one alive in the pool gets the remainder. It's like an annuity with lottery ticket, all in one!"

"Mhm," I mumbled, trying to read and listen. It sounded too good to be true, but since they had re-regulated the banking and insurance system again, there were lots of these investment schemes around. In many cases, the pitch included the notion that cutting out the banks and their greedy execs meant that all those savings could be shared with the investors. Sure.

He next sent reams of statistics about interest rates and costs of living which I mostly ignored. What did come burbling up in my mind was the old saying about return on capital being less of a concern than return *of* capital, and that reminded me of my precarious financial state.

"Oh, I think you'll be very pleased, and it doesn't take much to start, for example—" I still wasn't sure why he was telling me this, so I put my hand up to stop his recitation.

"Ranjit, what does this have to do with you and me?"

He appeared momentarily confused, like when you tell one of those religious types at the door you do not believe in God.

"Umm…sure…well. I need the extra credits, and this is such a good product," he said a tad nervously.

"Are you telling me you're selling this?"

"Yes of course…didn't I mention…and you can too, once you become an investor." He had that serious, anxious look. I stared at him thoughtfully, remembering the last time he came to me needing a favour. It ended up with me strapped to a table, my body being emptied of blood for the benefit of his Divine Life lover Zhang Lei.

"Whatever happened to Lei, by the way?" I interjected, wanting him to know I had not forgotten.

Ranjit had been twisting the tip of his moustache but stopped with my abrupt change of subject. "Hehe. Oh well you know. How are you feeling, Amir?" He avoided answering and the red flags started waving frantically in the back of my mind.

"I'm well, now. No thanks to your friend who would've drained me completely had it not been for the First Nations police who showed up in the nick of time." I had to get in my digs. Those two had almost killed me and now we were perma-banned from the reserve for blood trading.

"It was only blood. You can always make new. No harm done, right?"

"Sure. It wasn't you strapped to that table." The worst part was not that, but the sense of betrayal. My best friend was prepared to sacrifice me for his DL lover.

Ranjit shrugged. "I am terribly sorry. I swear I didn't know. You would've done the same."

"Nonsense! I would *not* have done the same."

Ranjit leaned away from me and held up his hands in mock surrender. "Amir, I already said I'm sorry." He had a look on his face that suggested he was sorry, but perhaps sorry for having met with me today. I sat there glaring at him as those memories once more poisoned my soul.

We said nothing for a few minutes. I, waiting for a truly sincere apology or an excuse to punch him. Then he sent me a thought. It was an offer of a significant discount on the investment.

"There. You can have it without my commission, if that pleases you," he said with a sour look. "I am doing this for you Amir. It is my way of…please accept this as my apology."

In truth, I too could use the extra credits. We had both

lived through the pension crisis and opted for a settlement that was little more than the universal basic income. "Ranjit, I have my home and some savings from the sale of antiques. Most everything else went to zero during the crash, as you know well."

He exhaled and nodded. "And that is why we must help each other. Believe me this investment is the best I've seen, and the extra monthly income will help us a lot."

"I can't afford to lose any savings. It's all I have, and no one will hire us, so it can't be replaced." I was looking in his eyes, struggling to gauge if he was telling the truth. We had been friends for decades. He worked in the financial side of government, me in research, so I was ill qualified for this decision. This would require trust, one damaged last time.

"I'm in the same situation and put in half my savings, and I've already received the first payment, right on schedule. Bought some Darjeeling tea with it," he grinned.

Ranjit has a tea fetish, and I tease him about it constantly, but I was happy he had been able to enjoy this small luxury. Then one of those selfish thoughts surfaced in the form of a what if? What if I had enough money for that trip to Africa I had been planning and never was able to afford. What if? I imagined it all as I sat there, how pleasant it would be, how perfect, and how deserved. I began smiling. He likely thought my smiles were about him. But it was the trip, a trip to visit my wife's grave, just once while I could.

It came out as a breath, like a wish made real by a virtual djinn. "I'll do it!"

"You will?" Ranjit sounded surprised. I suppose he had almost given up on his sales pitch. "That's grand!" he added, but with a look of incredulity.

"Yes. How do I start? I'll put in half my savings, but Ranjit, you must promise I won't lose it."

"This is gold-plated, Amir. I assure you. The credits are held in an annuity at a major bank and invested in the most secure mortgages and loans. Read the contract and agree to transfer the credits. It's as simple as that."

I did not bother reading it. Who does? In a few seconds, I was the proud owner of 1200 units of the Royal City Financial Group Tontine Annuity.

***

I recalled how happy I was when the first payment showed up in my bank account and I quickly did the math and realized it would only take eighteen months to accumulate enough for a ticket to Africa. I had spent the month cheerfully planning and looking at travel guides. But the second month's payment was now several days past due, and I was becoming concerned, so I contacted Ranjit. His response was curt. "Trying to locate Lei. Get back to you."

I had no idea what Lei had to do with my investment, so I sent another thought to Ranjit. No response this time. I was becoming very worried, so I went to the senior centre looking for him. He was not in, and the cheerful woman with the lisp who worked on the welcome desk said she had not seen him. I stood outside a few minutes later, at a complete loss.

Ranjit had told me he lived in the new complex by the park a block away, so I decided to go there in the off-chance I could get in. It was another of those printed buildings that looked like it had grown organically from a puddle of brown plastic mud. Many loved them, others did not. I was in the latter camp, but then I lived in a ninety-year-old house made of natural products like wood and stone which could no longer legally be obtained except in small amounts for the rich and for those of us needing essential repairs. At least the environmental protests had stopped with the shift to printing homes from human waste.

The entrance was set back from Woolwich Street to allow passenger drop-offs without impeding traffic. It let me in the foyer which apparently was changed daily displaying different scenes. Today must have been Neanderthal cave day, with scenes of water streaming down rocks into imaginary pools, and bats flitting on the ceiling. Very trendy. Ranjit told me the apartments had none of those old-fashioned, energy-wasting windows to the exterior. Instead, tenants could project scenes on the interior surfaces. He said his favourite in winter was a tropical beach complete with crabs scuttling and a large hammock hanging from a waving palm. He loved it and said he could swing while hooked up to his DL cradle that was re-imaged as the swing under the palm.

I was able to access the building AI. It said I was permitted to ring his apartment. I was surprised since people who live in these buildings often have many layers of security to shield themselves from others. But Ranjit did not, and I got through and heard his distinctive voice, "Ya, was expecting you Amir. Come in."

"Been avoiding me?" I said as the door swooshed shut.

Ranjit turned and walked away. "Busy," he muttered.

His apartment was not in beach mode though. It looked more like a command center on a star ship: dark, with glowing switches, read-outs, and mechanical things covering walls and ceiling over a riveted metal floor which clanged as I walked on it. His DL cradle was off to one side of what in my home is the living room. Here it was called a space, or something equally non-descriptive.

There was nowhere to sit but the metal floor and the cradle, so I chose the floor. His back to me, Ranjit fiddled with some screens filled with nonsensical graphs and data. I waited for him to speak. He knew why I was here.

"It's gone, Amir. It's all gone."

"I want my money back. So, whatever is gone had better not be my money."

"Fraid so, mine too." He turned to me and pointed to a spot in the floor. An ornate gold throne of antique Indian design appeared, perfectly complementing the reproduction Indian Maharajah outfit he was wearing. He regally settled on it and looked about as if for a servant with a fan.

"Your highness bought a spaceship?" I teased. He left me sitting uncomfortably on the floor. "Explain it…like you would to someone very old and stupid…like me."

"Did you not read the contract?"

"Course not. It was over forty pages. I assumed you did. Now where is my damned money?"

"It was supposed to be held in an annuity by Lei…in a bank—"

"Supposed? Lei?" I asked, my blood pressure monitor flashing red.

"Umm, yes. It seems to have gone sideways."

"What in hell does that mean? And why is Lei involved?"

The monitor was starting to intervene now, suffusing blood pressure lowering drugs into my bloodstream.

"I'm sorry Amir. I am caught in this too. Good thing I convinced you not to put in *all* your savings."

"You did not! That was my choice." I was starting to feel faint. Sadly, it is not easy to maintain outrage when your vitals are constantly being adjusted. But I did not want more drug intervention, so I closed my eyes and started a Buddhist chant to relax.

A few moments later when I opened my eyes, Ranjit was gone, along with all the visuals in the space. I found myself sitting on a white floor surrounded by plain white walls. I cursed Ranjit, my blood pressure again flirting with the red zone.

***

Ranjit had bugged out, leaving me to figure out what to do next. I was considering the possibilities on my way home. I had taken a minibus. It let me off near St. George's Square and I thought that instead of taking the connecting bus home, I would treat myself to a coffee and sweet. Surely, my health monitor would not object to that.

A generation ago, the soulless twentieth-century boxes surrounding the square were re-done in a neo-Victorian style which included all the modern tech. Most everyone but those emotionally stuck in the previous century approved.

It was a lovely early fall day, the first of the season's leaves decorating the grey-stone street with red and gold. I was sipping a heavenly brew when someone bumped me. Coffee spilled on my lap. My first reaction was fear, not about the coffee, but fear centered on the group of young brats who had surrounded my table and by the look on their faces, intent on mischief. "If you want credits, I have none," I said to them.

"All codgers have credits, don't they?" the one with the orange hat said as though it were an accepted fact.

I was about to tell them about my recent bad fortune, but I knew it would not matter to them in the slightest. "You're blocking the sun,' I said instead.

"That can be remedied," a girl who looked more like a boy stated.

"Then please remedy it." I knew they would not do anything illegal, because the surveillance AI was watching, and there would be police officers on stand-by near the square. But speaking to strangers was not illegal and they likely knew precisely how far they could go before the AI was triggered.

"Remedies often require credits, don't they?" the first boy said.

I seldom have brilliant ideas, but this day I did. "Are any of you lot in Divine Life?"

Most said no, but two nodded. "What of it?" the girl-boy said.

"If you want to make some credits, I might have a job for you."

***

More days went by and I battered Ranjit with constant thoughts. Nothing worked until I threatened to file a complaint with the Regional Investments AI. That got his attention since that AI often was in the news as having successfully prosecuted some mad scheme or other.

"I contacted Lei. He said it was all a misunderstanding.

Your credits should be back in your account soon," Ranjit eventually answered.

"When is soon? And you didn't answer me when I asked why Lei was involved."

"Soon is soon. And about the other thing...not on this channel. Can I come to your place? You don't have omni-surveillance, do you?"

"I have the minimum required by law. Come over this afternoon then."

***

I live in the West Core of Guelph, in a neighbourhood populated by people like me who bought before natural building products had been prohibited. Thereafter, as part of massive changes, property taxes had been abolished along with elected city governments. They were replaced by an AI and citizen assemblies appointed as needed to decide specific issues. It had worked reasonably well, but sometimes the AI was next to useless in dealing with matters not in its data range; and convening a citizen assembly to decide an issue was absurdly expensive and slow.

"I like your garden," Ranjit said.

"My wife laid it out when we moved here," I replied.

"She's been gone for decades and you still don't want to change it?"

"Something like that." I said, resenting his reference to that dark place in my pathetic life.

"Explains why it has the feel of an overgrown jungle."

"I am sure you are not here to critique my lack of gardening skills."

Ranjit twisted his moustache and carefully sat on the

painted wicker chair I offered him in the gazebo. "I have tea. Want some?" I said.

"Darjeeling?"

"No...manufactured. Waste fiber, tea flavouring, and caffeine, I think it said."

He made a face as though about to puke.

"Alright. We are safe here. I have the sound absorbers on. Now tell me what happened," I demanded.

"Nothing much to say. I trusted him."

"Still? After he lied to you about his identity and almost killed me?"

"I know. I feel like a fool." He steepled his fingers and leaned over like he wanted to speak to the gazebo floor. "The worst part was finding out he's a man. I loved her you know."

"Him."

Ranjit glanced up. I could see his eyes glistening. "Her in DL. He was she. And sucker that I am, I fell for her."

"Him...you fell in love with a man."

"Go ahead, rub salt in."

I was perched on the small ladder I had been using to paint the gazebo. "Sorry, Ranjit. But were there no tell-tales? Did she like to discuss soccer and drink craft beer?"

He shook his head.

"Hmm. So, you got burned. It happens. Then why did you get involved with him again?"

"Don't know. He just called...apologized...wanted to start again and—"

"And you fell for it twice?"

"Seems I am a twice-born sucker."

"Indeed. Now tell me how I get my money back."

"He said you will get it soon. I told you."

"If not?"

"Let us see what happens. Give him a chance."

"Are you insane? He gets no chances from me. If my credits are not back in my account in two days, he'll be sorry."

Ranjit looked around. "Be careful of making threats, Amir. They can be used—"

"I don't care if anyone hears. I have a Plan B and I assure you that he doesn't want me to use it."

"Plan B?"

"Yes. You said the money went sideways. Where is sideways?"

"That's just what Lei told me."

"I've been thinking about it a lot. Credits are easy to trace…if they stay within the system. But what if they don't? What if sideways is Divine Life? What if he converted our credits to DL dollars so he could live like a king in his virtual world?"

"You could be right."

"We need to run a trace and if it ends in DL, we'll know for sure. It's the only thing that makes sense. You said he practically lives in DL. Where else would he want the credits, but there?"

Ranjit smiled. "But if it is in Divine Life, how do we get it back?"

"My solution is Plan B. He has two days, no more, or I implement Plan B. Tell him that."

***

I did not expect my credits back in two days, but I needed the time to contact my brat friend and make a deal with her and her associates. Four of them agreed to my requirements. Now I just had to wait for the time limit to run out.

"I did the trace. Our credits went to the annuity. But without a court order, it wouldn't let me access what the annuity did with them," Ranjit thought to me.

"No courts. I consulted a law AI, sent it my contract. It promptly said I was screwed...in legalese, of course," I replied.

"Agreed. I did the same. It's a cleverly written document."

"Then it is down to Plan B?"

There was a pause, then he said, "Hmm. OK."

"I need his avatar name and the location of his home and hangouts in DL."

He sent it moments later. "What is Plan B, Amir?"

"I can't tell you. Secrecy is important. You have to trust me."

"I do, but—"

"You don't have to worry, I can't do him any bodily harm in DL, it's just pixels and stuff."

"Alright," he thought to me along with a smiley face emoji.

***

Three days later, Zhang Lei showed up in person at my door. I said the word to my home, setting it to high alert. Lei was dressed simply in a brown robe that made him look like a penitent monk. "We need to talk," he said.

"I want my money," I replied.

"I want mine too."

That piqued my interest, so I had home security scan him for weapons. There were none. I ushered him in to the living room.

"Nice antiques," he said.

"They weren't antique when I bought them. Now tell me what's going on before I report you to the authorities."

Lei bowed. "Out of respect, I fear this is about Ranjit and me and you are collateral damage."

"What do you mean?"

"You didn't read that contract, did you?"

"Doesn't matter. I want my credits back."

"Amir, please pull up the document and search for my name."

I did. His name was not there. I was confused.

"Now search Ranjit's name."

It was near the end in the document. It clearly stated that Ranjit was the owner of the Royal City Financial Group Tontine Annuity where my credits were to be deposited. "What in the name—" I blurted.

"Precisely. Ranjit has our credits. He suckered me as well, then had double revenge by having your griefer brats destroy my DL."

| 3 |

Chapter Three

A month had passed since Ranjit made off with half my savings. I could ill afford to lose anything, never mind that much. There were rumours he was camped in some mountain village in northern India. But I had no solid leads; leaving me with simmering anger and worry that I might lose my home. There was one benefit, however. I could occupy my spare time imagining clever ways to murder him without being caught. I would never do it, of course, but the scenarios were amusing and eased the feelings of helplessness. Along with that psychological load, I felt bad about having turned Zhang Lei's Divine Life experience into griefer hell. I offered some credits to him so he could start again with a new avatar, but he waved away the suggestion and said he would get me another time, whatever that meant.

"Got anymore work for me, Amir?" It was Darwina, the brat girl who had helped me with my problem with Lei. I did not recognize her at first because she had done something strange to her hair and lips.

"Don't think so," I said. I was seated at my favourite Iraqi cafe in St. George's Square, sipping thick coffee, properly served in an antique silver dallah.

Darwina did not leave, so I offered to share.

"Gives me the shakes," she said, refusing.

"Would you prefer tea?"

"That would be nice. Jiaogulan, if they have it."

I sent a thought to the server and received an instant response. "They have it," I told her.

"Are you pleased with our work in DL?"

"Umm…you were very effective," I said, being evasive.

"We haven't seen his avatar since."

"I know."

The young waiter brought the tea in a lovely ceramic cup with leafy tendrils painted around the lip. Years ago, everyone had tried robots as service workers, but they were too slow and lacked the ability to adapt to accents and speech patterns. Then it became far cheaper to use humans, since many would pay for the privilege of working.

"Thank you," Darwina said after the waiter had left.

I looked at her again. "I like your new…umm…hair."

"It's the latest. My lips too. See?"

Her hair had a natural tight curl that shimmered in waves of iridescent colour much like some insect wings. Her mouth was the same in pattern.

"Must have cost a lot."

"That's how I used your credits."

"Ahh. well spent," I said flattering her, although in truth I had no strong feelings about fashions.

"Are you sure you don't have more work for me?" she said, blowing on her hot tea.

I thought a moment. She seemed a nice girl, despite her attempted shake-down last time and her ready willingness to grief strangers online. "Hmm. Do you like manual labour?"

"I don't do sex with men, if that's what you mean."

"Not at all. How about gardening?"

"Explain."

"I have a backyard that's a bit overgrown. It needs trimming, weeding, so on."

"You look healthy for a codger. Can you not do that?"

"I can but it's not my preference."

"Never done gardening, but I can try."

"It's easy but tiring."

"Why don't you hire a company?"

"Can't afford it. And you are wrong about codgers. Most of us aren't rich, far from it in fact."

She smiled. A wave of fly wing colours flickered over her mouth. "I know. We say that because it seems wrong to take money from poor old people. So, we pretend you are all rich."

"I can't afford to pay much."

She nodded then seemed to be listening to something from her implant. "I have one condition," she said.

"Yes?"

"I need a temporary place to stay. Been couch surfing and just got booted."

"Hmm. Just for a few days then, while you work on my garden. I have a spare bedroom and bathroom in the basement."

"Perfect!"

"But no stealing and no friends over to visit. Understand?"

"Agreed. And for you…no touching and no sex."

"No worries. Give me access to your ID. I want to verify that you are not underage nor have a problematic history."

She smirked. "I need yours too, for the same reason."

We exchanged info. She was nineteen and clean, a pleasant surprise. "Here is my address. You can start tomorrow," I said.

***

The woman was one of those natural blonds with strikingly white skin, not porcelain white but the kind that is almost transparent. She said her name is Nora. "Just moved in and noticed you outside with that boy trimming shrubs. Not many people around, so I thought I'd drop over and introduce myself."

"Welcome to the neighbourhood," I said, my heart filling my throat.

"My grandparents lived here. When they passed, I inherited. Didn't know what to do with it. It's a bit of a heap."

"Ah yes, I remember them...June and Peter?"

"You knew them?"

"Not really. Would wave hello sometimes. He liked to help his neighbours with that ancient snowblower."

"Yep, that's him...my grandpa Peter. Brought that blower down from the north."

Darwina was dragging a large tree branch out of the backyard. "Your relation?" Nora asked.

"No, a girl I hired for yard work. Nothing more, I assure you," I said, embarrassed that I felt the need to explain.

"Ahh a girl. Should've guessed from the hair. It's sizzling-hot now."

I shrugged. Nora looked the career type with regulation

outerwear that suggested nothing, all forms of self-expression having been banned from the workplace. "You work?" I asked.

"I do. For Xaltanium…an integration imagineer."

"I see," I said because I did not want an explanation.

"Just moved from up north. Just started my new job then got a summons. Very annoying. I need to get to work on the house before it caves in."

"A summons?"

"One of those citizen assemblies. Why couldn't they have picked someone else?"

"Random selection by the AI. Don't take it personally. Do you know your topic or how many on your assembly?"

"Nope. I have to show up at City Hall for a briefing."

"There are ways to get out of it."

"I'm not pregnant, nor sick. I forget the rest of the reasons. Looked it up, but none apply."

"Too bad. Maybe it will be interesting."

Nora rolled her eyes. I did not blame her. Serving was obligatory and necessary. But few would volunteer, given the choice.

"Alright, must go. Do you mind if I invite you and your little friend over once I clear a space in the dining room?"

"Be my pleasure," I responded and meant it.

"Who was that extra-white woman?" Darwina said, after Nora had left.

"Her name is Nora. Just moved in across the street."

"Lucky you."

"Don't be silly."

"I mean she improves the view."

"Maybe for you," I teased.

"I saw your face. Your eyes were painting her, tip to toes."

"Alright, you win. She is…well…exotic that's for sure and…never mind. How is the trimming going?"

Darwina had been with me for two days. I was not sure I had done the right thing since I had not lived with anyone in decades since my wife died. But Darwina had been quiet and helpful, said she enjoyed the calm and security. It was only a few more days, I told myself, and the backyard already was looking much better.

"It's going well back there," she answered." Like me to make supper?"

"You know how to cook?" I replied with a chuckle that must have offended her.

"Amir, I have parents. I went to school. I can take care of myself, and that includes cooking. Do you want supper or not?"

"Apologies. Go ahead. I appreciate it."

It turned out she was barely passable as a cook, having burned the kale somehow and undercooked the quinoa. But with the addition of lots of spicy sauce, it was edible.

"Saw Nora again. She looked upset," Darwina mumbled, her shimmery lips sucking in the last of the slippery kale.

"Oh?"

"Might want to check on her," she grinned, "or I could."

"Leave it to me."

"She seems perfect for a do-good codger."

"Brat!"

"You are one of those ReGen riders, aren't you?"

"I am. Why do you ask?"

"You don't look that old, except your eyes."

"They are original, that's why."

"How old are you then?"

"You have my ID. Do the math if you can."

She made a rude gesture with her finger, then consulted her AI for the answer. "Wow!" she said under her breath, "128?"

"Just…last month."

"Can you still get it up?"

"Yes, but there's no point."

"Funny!"

"And how about you? Why are you couch surfing?"

She turned her head away and said, "What do you have for sweets?"

"Nothing but honey…and you didn't answer me."

"Oh, the usual. I really am a brat. Ask my parents and those pervs who run the youth shelter."

"There is always work."

"For me? Are you serious? People pay a lot to get decent jobs. Two year's salary in many cases."

"That's how it's been since automation took over," I noted. "You have no sponsor?"

"I'm a brat, remember? No one will sponsor me. I'm too much trouble."

"You are doing a fine job here."

"You've only known me for a few days."

"Alright but leave the silverware and china. Those were my grandparents. Worth nothing these days. Even the charities won't take them. But they remind me—"

"If you warn me not to steal again, I *will* steal them."

"You are definitely a brat."

Darwina stood suddenly, antique silver cutlery clattering to the floor. "Someone's coming!" she said.

"How—"

"I'm in your house security. Got visuals now. It's Nora. You'd better greet her."

I opened the door in time for Nora to slip past into the foyer. "I brought a welcoming pie. Look," she said.

It was indeed a pie but stuck on top was a paper note on which was written. *Need help. Turn off AI. Turn on sound absorbers. Please!*

"Thank you for the pie," I said, taking it from her and handing it to Darwina. Then I did as she asked and locked the door. "We are secure now. What's up?" I said.

"I'm so sorry. I have no one else. Are you sure no one is listening?"

"Think so, although my neighbour across the street is a bit nosey," I teased.

She smiled that smile. My mind filled with memories. "Careful," Darwina whispered to me, then said in loud voice, "Come in Nora. I'll make some tea."

"Remember I told you about my summons?" Nora said after she had parked her shapely bottom on my priceless Ikea leather Poang chair.

"Yes, the citizen assembly."

"I went to the orientation. The topic for consultation has to do with building a new main library—"

I snorted.

"Something wrong?"

"They've been debating that for decades. Even decided in 2019 to build it. Then the pandemic and depression hit, and it was cancelled, and—"

"Yes, I know. They briefed us."

"And?"

"And there are nineteen in our assembly to decide this question."

I nodded.

"And you said we were selected at random."

"Yes. The number in the assembly is optimized by the AI for the question under study and membership is a random selection from eligible voters."

"So, you say. Maybe so, but something isn't right."

Darwina had returned with the tea and some stale cookies she found. "There are rumours on the street," Darwina said pouring the tea.

"What isn't right?" I asked.

"Well, what do you think are the chances of having several people on the Assembly who know each other...I mean personally?"

"Hmm. Not high. Guelph has over half a million people and most can vote."

"Precisely. Furthermore, do you think it probable that the ones who know each other all want to demolish the old library and sell the land?"

"Knew it!" Darwina exclaimed.

I looked at them both. Something was missing, and that something was a logical explanation. "Could be chance. It's possible to flip several heads in a row, you know." They both threw me confused looks. "The old metal currency. That's how they...never mind. We must not rule out chance, is all I'm saying."

"Chance has been very kind to the rich for a very long time," Darwina said, her sarcasm clear.

"Alright, I accept it could be chance, but what about this?" Nora's eyes flickered as she consulted her AI. "Hmm. It's gone. What the—"

"They deleted something, didn't they?" Darwina said.

Nora stopped what she was doing with her AI. Her eyes narrowed on Darwina. "How did you know?"

"Conspiracies. It's what street people talk about when we aren't...umm...you know."

The women had stopped talking and I assumed they were sending thoughts to each other. "Excuse me, but I live here too. What the hell is going on?"

"Oh, sorry Amir. Bad habit, and this is scary. You sure no one can hear us?" Nora asked again, her quivering hand giving away her nerves.

"Your thought messages are all saved somewhere, you know...much less safe than speaking here," I replied.

"That's what we were discussing. Is it possible for thought messages to be deleted?" Nora asked.

"Not likely. There are backups, and so on," I said.

"Nonsense!" Darwina blurted.

"Alright, let's not argue. Were you going to share a message with us, Nora?"

"It's gone. I tried to trace it."

"What was it about?" I asked.

"It was...oh my, am I going mad?"

"They offered a bribe and a threat, didn't they?" Darwina said as though it was a daily occurrence.

"They said if I vote to demolish and sell, I will receive free ReGen treatments for life. Otherwise, my life may be shorter than anticipated...something like that."

"That's crazy," I said.

"No, that's how decisions are made nowadays," said Darwina.

"Nora, did anyone else receive this generous offer?" I asked.

"Don't think so. But I overheard one in the group supporting demolition whisper, "She was supposed to be with us." Then another replied, "Stupid AI." We had a preliminary vote and I abstained. I seem to be the deciding ballot. Minutes later, I received the offer."

"We need to get you out of that Assembly," Darwina said firmly.

***

"We've already been over it. She has no valid reason to be excused," I said, my voice tainted with annoyance. Nora had decided to stay the night for security. She was still asleep in the spare bedroom upstairs.

"They are too powerful," Darwina said as though saying it made it fact.

I grimaced. We had been up half the night, and I was irritable from lack of sleep.

"You know we left the sound absorbers on all night. People do that when they are having sex," Darwina giggled for the first time since she'd arrived.

I decided to ignore her innuendo. "This could be a good

thing, as I said last night. Maybe after reviewing the facts, she'll agree that demolition and sale is best, and she'll get Re-Gen treatments thrown in for free."

Darwina sighed loudly. "It's a matter of principle, Amir. When political parties and elections were abolished, some parties didn't just go away. They went underground."

"You and your stupid conspiracy theories," I said, noting my cranky tone.

"Stupid codger," Darwina muttered.

We were cleaning up breakfast when Nora floated down the stairs in a pink floral nightdress, her blond hair flowing, her pink lips dazzling, her translucent skin radiant. Darwina punched my arm so hard it went numb.

Nora gazed at us through reddened eyes then scrunched up her face and sneezed, spraying snot everywhere. "Damned dust," she mumbled between sniffles. "I'm beginning to hate these old houses."

For some reason, Darwina thought that hilarious, especially when Nora temporarily became naked as her smart outfit changed textures and shape as it morphed into her business uniform. "That one has a HUD?" she asked Nora.

"Yes. One I designed, in fact."

"Ahh, that's what you do," I said, understanding at last.

Nora pulled out a chair at the breakfast table. "Alright, what are my options?" she said.

"Synth eggs or granola," Darwina answered, pouring her some coffee.

"I don't eat breakfast. I mean what are my options for that damned assembly. It was all a jumble last night when I went to bed."

"I think we settled on three options," I said. "I'll have the eggs, Darwina."

"They are by the stove."

I looked at her thinking that if I were young, blond, and female, cooked eggs would appear magically on my plate. I set that vain wish aside and turned back to Nora. "If you remember, option one involved leaving Guelph and moving back to Wawa. That would make you ineligible to serve on the assembly."

Nora shook her head and carefully sniffed the coffee, "And make me a coward."

"Or prudent, depending one's perspective."

"A coward is a coward," Nora grumbled. "What are the other options again?"

I held up my fingers and started counting them off. "We eliminated lodging a complaint, because of lack of proof. Next you could just accept their offer and be done with it—"

Nora's face grimaced, "Forget that one, I'm no sell-out."

"Then we are down to our third option...vote your conscience and take the consequences."

"Do you think they would actually do anything to me?"

Darwina banged the coffee pot on the counter, "Nora, be sensible! Any group who can rig an AI and delete messages from secure servers are quite capable. People even go missing, and—"

"Enough! Option three is a non-starter. Not work the risk." Nora tapped her head. "There is a fourth. Thought about it while trying to get to sleep."

"Not the one about me dressing up as a redhead, I hope," Darwina snorted.

"That was a joke," Nora grinned. "But we can play dress-up some other time."

I almost choked and noticed a blush on Darwina's dark cheeks. "Uh huh...well back to the topic, shall we?"

"Indeed," Nora said, eyes flicking through her makeup HUD display. "Confusing interfaces deter use. That's a maxim in our business. People need simple and intuitive. What-if...what-if I made me confusing?"

"Meaning?"

"Meaning, I will not be easy to use. I will give contradictory views. I will not be in one camp nor the other."

"To what end? It will only delay the process," I noted.

"Precisely. Delay is a perfectly acceptable solution. Drive them mad with indecision. Be a ditzy blond. Forget everything from one day to the next."

"And smile sweetly so they don't strangle you," Darwina added.

"You got it! I looked it up. The time limit for the assembly is three months. I can do that, and the pay isn't bad. If there is no decision, the assembly is dissolved."

"You still risk more threats and inducements," I said.

"Thought of that too...installed a keyword trap. Messages that trigger it are automatically saved to this drive." Nora held up her hand and pointed to the gold ring on her finger. "No deleting those files without my finger and eye print."

"An old memory ring...how clever. You are amazing, Nora," Darwina gushed. I felt like punching her arm.

| 4 |

Chapter Four

"I went to see the main library," Nora said, watching us adding leaves to the composter. She had come dressed in pristine blue overalls and faux leather work boots but had yet to let anything soil them. She was our garden ornament. We did not mind. "The building is sealed in enviro-wrap," she added.

"Yes, they did that seven…eight years ago, I think," I explained.

"They don't care about the building. It's the contents," Darwina muttered loud enough so we could hear.

"I'm glad you're done with it," I said.

"Yes, it took far less that I imagined. Only a week of blondness and they were begging for mercy."

I laughed. "You let them off easy."

"I know. I took their second offer…that I be released from service because of diminished mental capacity. Hope it doesn't go on my record."

"Solves the problem for Nora but not our city," Darwina muttered again, sounding like she was swearing at us under her breath.

"What do you mean?" I asked.

Darwina stopped gathering leaves. "Mean? Isn't it obvious?"

After a week with her, I knew her slant. "If you mean the AI will correct it's mistake...it obviously will."

"And a bogus study will be done, and the majority will vote to demolish and sell," Darwina finished the logic as she saw it.

"I thought of that Darwina. But what could I do? You told me I couldn't resist them, that it was too dangerous."

"It will take an equally strong group to oppose them," Darwina mused.

"I still don't know why the library is so controversial that lives are threatened because of it."

Darwina glanced up, "It contains the archives, that's why."

"But the archives must've been digitized generations ago," Nora said.

"Everyone knows digital copies can't be trusted. They can be hacked and altered. It's the physical ones, the originals they are after." Darwina explained unnecessarily.

"Amir, what do you think might be in those archives?" Nora asked.

"Newspapers, documents, contracts, studies...that kind of thing. All moved back from the museum when they needed space for more exhibits."

"And all of it dusty paper, I'll bet." Nora said looking like she was about to sneeze just from the mention of it.

"More likely they are dusty microfiches," I said, noticing both were consulting AIs.

"They copied the newspapers and documents on rolls of photographic film," Nora was the first to find it.

"Yes, and they had these huge microfiche readers last time I was in there," I said.

"You were in there?" a surprised Darwina asked.

"Just said so, didn't I? And yes, it was the main library. It changed a lot, over time. Initially it was all paper and people then it became photographic and electronic, then finally digital and internet. Then the troubles came and there was no point going there in person. Everything could be accessed online."

Darwina leaned her rake on the gazebo. "My friends say the important archives are the newspapers."

"Indeed. When the newspapers closed, the paper copies were donated to the library, microfiched, then destroyed."

Nora had been listening carefully. "All very interesting," she said, "but we still don't know why the fuss over a bunch of dusty microfiches."

"I was joking about the dust. It should be pristine in there with all the environmental controls."

"Hmm, then suitable for a visit?"

"It's sealed," I reminded her.

Nora shrugged.

"Nora, did you discover why that group in the assembly wants to demolish and sell the library?" Darwina asked.

"Ah…ah…" Nora's face was about to explode when Darwina pressed a big maple leaf under her nose.

"Gaaa…filthy leaves!" Nora snorted it away, then started to laugh. "Well, I'm…I'm no gardener that's for sure."

"In the old days, we burned leaves to get rid of them. Much less work and the smell amazing."

They looked at me like I was mad.

***

We had resolved nothing except to give it a rest and thank our lucky stars that ill had not befallen us. Sometimes that is the best one can do with life. And the yard work was done too, and I was vacillating about what to do about Darwina. She had been stimulating company, to say the least, with all her conspiracy theories and wacky ideas. But I could not afford to keep her either.

"The pantry sent an order to your provider," Darwina said, passing me on the stairs to the basement.

"Oh, alright."

"You want to kick me out, don't you?"

"No, no…well…umm."

"Just say it and I will go."

"Where?"

"Somewhere."

"Such as?"

"I think I'll live with Nora and help reno her house."

"Really?"

"No, not really. Teasing. Prefer it here, actually."

"I'm sorry Darwina, I can't afford to keep you."

"Is that all? You need credits?"

"I can barely—"

"And I thought it was because of my…you know."

"I don't want sex, Darwina. I may look forty, but my mind is more mature than that."

"Hmm. I can pay now. Something happened last month. Fixed now."

"OK." I sent her an estimate. "This is how much you cost."

"I'll pay double…for upkeep. Can I keep my room?"

"Let's try it for a month. If we want to kill each other after that—"

"I'll leave peacefully, if that is your worry."

"Deal!"

"You may give me a hug, roomie."

It was an onerous task. I sighed. She giggled.

***

"I need a consult, now!" Nora said so loudly even the neighbour's security AI must have heard.

"Alright," I replied, wondering what she wanted.

Darwina greeted Nora with a peck on the cheek.

"It's urgent and private, Nora said then nodded in the direction of my security panel. I turned off the house AI and so on.

"They contacted me again, and I caught them in my trap." Nora flashed us her ring as she went to the kitchen.

"What did they say? And who is they? And why you again? And—"

Nora held up her hand to stop Darwina's incessant flow of questions. I smiled. Yes, she could be that annoying. "How the…?"

"They wiped your ring archive, didn't they?" Darwina said, a bemused look forming.

Nora's slightly hateful glance halted Darwina from further mocking.

"I had family pics in there...Gramma and Grampa at the beach. Oh...f..."

"Sorry Nora," we said.

"Those bastards! I was ready to walk away, my reputation compromised, and now this. I'll not let them get away with deleting my grandparents."

I was taken aback by her flaming vehemence, the level of which I knew could lead to rash behaviour. "Careful, Nora. They may be bating you."

Darwina disagreed. "No, I think they didn't know what you had on them, so they decided to delete your back-up drive. They likely didn't even know where it was till you used it to store their malware message."

"Then why didn't my malware program detect it?"

Darwina pulled a curl of her freshly back-to-original hair, "Hard to know. Maybe their malware was too new or so old it was no longer in the database."

"You asked awhile ago if I'd discovered the reason why they wanted to demolish and sell the library. I didn't answer on purpose...wanted it over. But this is too much. I surrendered and they decided to harm me anyway."

"People like that are arrogant. They mock us and think we'll do nothing because we cling like suckling piglets to our universal basic income," said Darwina, appearing even more heated than Nora.

"Wait!" I shouted. "We can be as seditious as we want in here, but the moment it leaves our home, we'll bring the authorities down on our heads. Never forget they are watching."

Darwina gave me the finger of disrespect.

"Childish protest doesn't work either," I chided.

"But revenge might," Nora said with a conspiratorial glint. "Now let me tell you what I learned while in the assembly."

***

"Don't look at the library directly," I said. "We're just gliders, remember."

"I hate gliding, makes me nauseous," Darwina complained.

"It's good for you Darwina," Nora said, all kitted out in the latest gear. "I'm glad we rented these."

"And the metal diffuser patch was a good idea," I said, "as long as it sticks to the skin and covers your ID implant."

"And I hope everyone has turned off all apps," Nora said between breaths.

Darwina grumbled, "Gliding without shopping is even less fun."

"You sure no one can hear us?" I asked while we waited to cross the street.

"Our ID implants are blocked, so they would have to be close enough to hear our voices the old-fashioned way," Darwina explained.

Nora looked at her.

"Ears, Nora, with their ears."

"Alright you two. Pay attention. The building is sealed but for the HVAC inlet/outlet on the roof. See that grey box? That's it." I stopped myself from pointing at it.

Nora covered her mouth before saying, "How does that help? We would end up inside it and this time of the year it's in heating mode."

'Let's glide this way," Darwina pointed down the section of Paisley Street that goes past the library. "See that re-seal-able side door?" she whispered as we went past. "It's where the maintenance guy enters."

"And I suppose you know him?" Nora asked.

"Nope. I know his sister."

"Looks like it has a hand-eye reader, so the sister won't do," I said.

"Let's go home and game this in a more secure place," Nora whispered. "Rattles my nerves talking out here."

***

"Before we waste time planning an illegal break-in, lets take a minute to discuss why we care about any of this," I said.

They were selecting makeup and accessories again and Nora must have closed her HUD because her eyes lowered to mine. "For me it's personal. But I take your point. This could be needlessly risky."

"Or a setup," Darwina added.

Nora nodded. "Thought about that too. But I'm having a hard time letting go."

"Because of that message you got by mistake at the assembly meeting?" I asked.

Nora looked out my back door to the garden. "You two did a nice job."

"You helped," Darwina said.

"Pfft. No, I didn't...but I did look good in that outfit, didn't I?"

"Fetching," Darwina flirted.

"Your outfit was functional," I said, "but we still don't know what that message meant."

"It was about cleaning up *origins*...that it was imperative," Darwina repeated what Nora had told us earlier.

"When they thought I was with them. But we still don't know for sure what *origins* means. So even if we could get in the library, we wouldn't know what to look for."

"Could be anything," a pang of guilt stabbing my conscience as soon as I said it.

Darwina dropped the bowl of synth-eggs in front of me. "Amir don't be so thick. Everyone knows."

"Sure, everyone meaning you and your reputable friends?"

"At least they're friends," she countered.

"Don't want you two lovers breaking up over this," Nora teased. "But Amir, honestly it makes more sense than anything else we've come up with."

"We didn't get here by accident," Darwina said.

"You two aren't old enough to remember how bad it was. No one with half a brain wants to go back to that," I said, my spoon making circles in the unappetising mush Darwina had made.

"We lost our freedom and democracy, and now they are erasing how it happened," Darwina said, practising her protest.

"Have you considered that it might be for the best?" I asked.

"Amir, are you implying there might be some validity to Darwina's theories?"

I sighed. "You don't understand, Nora. We came to hate partisan politics. We voted to end it."

"Just checked. Wikipedia says it was by popular demand...hmm...that we evolved to a higher form...etc.," Darwina read.

"Not exactly true, is it, Amir?" Nora had stopped admiring the garden and turned to face us, her face determined, her outfit changed to industrial grey.

"No...but we've had decades of stability, since."

Darwina's face changed to angry. "At what cost? You know why we despise codgers and riders, don't you? It's largely because they want stability and longevity and don't care how it affects the rest of us."

"Back to that erroneous trope?" I asked, my tone sarcastic.

Nora sighed. "Can we keep this civil? Amir, what could be in the library about *origins* that needs to be cleaned up?"

"If we could get in there....and we can't, the first place I would look is in the newspaper microfiches of that period," I suggested, the heat of embarrassment flushing my face.

"Why?" they both said.

"I...I voted for them. I know who did it."

They wanted an explanation and I provided it as best I could. We had political parties and elections back then, except in some municipalities where parties already had been banned. It was a divisive, disturbing time, and it made no logical sense to extend human life using ReGen treatments in a deeply unhappy world. More were opting for suicide than life extension, it was that bad, until the idea emerged somewhere in America and spread like wildfire around the world. It offered a permanent end to the chaos. Within a decade, the parties promoting it had swept to power most everywhere. They enacted legislation handing the running of society to law AI's guided by randomly selected citizen assemblies. But most of us remained suspicious, so political parties and elections remained for a time. Historians called this the laughocracy period. We still had elected politicians, but they had become costly, useless entertainment, much like the royal families of previous eras. Ultimately, partisan elections were banned, and we settled into the society we have today.

"In the end, democracy dies when partisan passion burns goodwill to ashes," I concluded, quoting a popular phrase of the time.

"But did it die a natural death or was it murdered?" Nora mused.

"*You* voted to end democracy?" Darwina asked in her best accusatory voice.

"That kind of it, yes. More than ninety percent of us did," I said, trying to defend my choice.

"Tell us specifically what we will find in that library," Nora demanded.

"How it was not a spontaneous uprising. How it was managed, step-by-step. It was more an assisted death than a natural one, Nora," I responded.

"And no one tried to stop them?"

"At first many…then they would ratchet up the chaos."

Nora nodded. "And who is *they*?"

"The party who ultimately benefited. The one who still runs things. The one who can rig the assembly and erase messages," I admitted.

"Has it occurred to you that it will not satisfy them to erase the written records? They must also eliminate those who remember," Nora mused.

"We are too few for them to care, and once the records are gone, there will be no proof," I said.

Darwina nodded. "And they will claim the ReGen treatments have muddled your minds."

"That too," I agreed.

"Then what shall we do?" Nora asked.

Darwina answered first. "We need to get in the library to access the microfiche records. They will confirm what Amir said about the past, and once we have proof—"

"It will change nothing. They won long ago. There's no going back," I said.

"There's no going forward either. They've taken away our ability to change the future. We are locked in place."

We sat for a moment silent in our fears and worries. I, because of the past and my role in it, they because of a future they cannot control.

I pushed away my uneaten synth eggs. "I'll help you, but you must promise me one thing. The way forward must be on a path of peace and moderation. We must not set our community aflame."

Darwina made a joke about anarchist bomb plans she had found somewhere, and Nora quipped that moderation has always been her thing while changing to a crazy ninja outfit replete with weapons. "I will smite our opponents," she crouched, grinning and ready to spring.

We had a good laugh, underlaid with tacit agreement to continue. "We can start with that building maintenance guy,"

Darwina said after the joking had ended. "Nora, do you mind if I offer you as bait?"

"Sure. One date for one entry into the library," Nora smiled sweetly.

"We are getting ahead of ourselves. Let's find out if he can get into the area where the archives should be located and if security can be turned off," I said.

"I can handle that," Darwina offered.

"We have a more immediate problem. They are monitoring us. We'll need a good reason to continue messing with AIs and sound absorbers. It's likely we've already have been flagged," I said.

Darwina snapped her fingers and grinned. "I heard having a sex club is perfectly legit."

"Oh Darwina!" I chuckled.

The women laughed. Darwina added, "See, he isn't completely dead. But seriously, it's a brilliant idea. We can announce it to the listeners next time Nora comes over."

"I'll be sure to change the sheets," I told them. They both gave me one of those looks that meant I had no chance.

***

Several days passed. Darwina had contacted the maintenance guy and was trying to convince him to join us. Then later she informed us that he is gay, so unless I was willing to date him, we would need other inducements other than Nora. We were at an impasse.

It was after midnight. An urgent thought message from Nora woke me. "Get Darwina. Go outside immediately," she said.

The night sky glowed orange. Many had joined us on the

street. "It's in the Core. Must be an old church," someone said. "No, it has to be one of the food vendors on Quebec Street," said another. The smell reminded me of smoldering leaves but with an acrid note of something unnatural.

"Look at the local news feed," Darwina whispered to us.

"It's the library. The library is burning!" Nora cried.

| 5 |

Chapter Five

"His name is Neep," explained Darwina, "and I think he means to speak with you."

"I seldom accept friend requests from dogs," I replied.

"You should this time. He is with Nora." I knew Darwina was about to taunt me again about the thing I had for Nora, so I gave her a warning look.

"Alright, your loss. He's an interesting old codger...much like you actually."

"Thanks, Darwina."

We were standing in the rock garden that used to be my driveway in the era of self-owned cars. The dog had stopped staring at me and was sniffing my shoe.

"Be careful, he sometimes—"

The dog called Neep swivelled his little turnip-coloured body and lifted his hind leg.

"What the—" I cried.

"That's what you get for ignoring him. Should've accepted his friend request." That belated advice was delivered with a garnish of giggles.

"Oh alright, damned dogs. They're either opinionated grumps, or idiotic nags."

"As I said, much like you." Darwina had her curly dark hair tied to look like poodle ears and she must have upgraded her lip texture HUD because she was displaying drool. She could be funny when she was not trying to blow up the world.

I scrolled back through my messages and reluctantly accepted Neep's friend request. Almost instantly my feed was filled with a low whine followed by repeated demands to be picked up.

"He wants to smell you," Darwina said. Next came a face from her suggesting I had better do as ordered. So, I bent down, fully expecting to be bitten, but instead the little fellow jumped into my hands. By the time I was upright again he'd inhaled most of me, and by the happy look on his face and the near constant "Yup, yup," from him in my implant, he seemed well pleased by what he'd smelled.

"We'd best use conference call. Dogs understand our speech but can't communicate except using thoughts translated by the AI," Darwina explained.

"I know. I was here a long time ago when it was invented, as you keep reminding me."

"Och, Whaur hae ye bin walkin'?" Neep said in what sounded like a Highland Scots accent.

"What's with the strange voice?" I asked him.

"Am a Cairn terrier. Nora prefers mah Scots self," Neep said, wiggling in my arms.

Darwina giggled again. "I kind of like it too. Told her he needs a wee kilt."

"He would pee on it," I said, ever practical.

Neep thought back to us, "Ye hink aam glaikit?"

"No idea what you mean. Speak proper English or I'll un-friend you." I said, confirming Darwina's opinion of me.

Neep looked at me, his furry head tilted to one side, mouth closed, body tense. "You don't like foreign accents?"

"The essence of communication is to be understood. Now can I let you down?"

"You could turn on your translator," the little dog argued.

Darwina smirked. I was being bested by a dog and she evidently was enjoying that. "Set it to auto-translate. You should be fine. But you'll miss most of his wit in translation."

"Last thing I need right now is a dog comedian."

"Aww, poor Amir. Life getting you down?"

"No more than usual, and what've you been up to?" I set Neep carefully on the sidewalk and he instantly trotted to the grassed boulevard for a pee.

"Helping Nora with her house."

"And?"

"And she wants it restored to original, but the engineer said that was near impossible since many of the materials used back then have been banned or no longer manufactured."

"The roof is the worst."

"Yep. That old solar installation is a heap of toxic plastic. Will cost a fortune to dispose of it."

"Had to deal with the same issues over the years," I said. "That's what keeps me broke. Always something to fix and it's seldom cheap and easy."

"Try living without a home."

"Well you have one now…sort of."

"You'll tire of me. They always do. Anyway, I'd better get back to work."

"Yeah, I have a ReGen appointment. Better go too."

Neep had been unusually quiet. I scanned the street for him.

"I think he went in your house," Darwina said as she waved to leave.

"Damned dog! Get out of there!" I yelled at him.

***

The nearby ReGen lab was in the old industrial area off Imperial Road, re-purposed like almost everywhere and everyone. No one wanted to live there because of fears of what might lie underground, so it had been surface cleaned, a garden planted, and transparent buildings on stilts installed above. It was a grand solution, since the gardens below had become a favourite with the locals, including me.

"Nice view isn't it?" Doctor Allan Tattie said.

"Indeed. You can see the closed factories and abandoned airport from here," I quipped.

"Ever the optimist," Tattie noted, his protruding eyes scanning the tablet. "I see you need a minor tune-up, blood cleaning and skin scrub."

"Already?"

"It's been a few months. You are overdue. Hmm. Good thing your plan was grandfathered. I see they increased the price again."

"I was one of the first to enrol. That's why I can't miss a payment...bought the locked-in price option."

"Then consider yourself fortunate, few can afford it now."

"Indeed. Back then they assumed in their business plan that everyone would want to live longer."

Tattie chuckled, "Would you if you had my body?"

He was right of course, but I made no comment. That insolent dog I had met earlier was not the only one who reminded me of a turnip, or in my doctor's case, a potato.

"Then the religions objected that it wasn't part of God's plan, and then the over-population activists had a go, then—"

"I know. Then the government pulled funding for ReGen when their pension actuaries reminded them the escalating costs would sink us."

"Not sure that was true though."

"Nor I. But it's done and sentiment quickly turned against us."

"Then let us hope you live a *very* long time."

I knew he said that to all his patients. I smiled at him, playing my role, in-turn. "And what kind of torture have you planned for me today?"

"We'll start with the blood cleaning. You know where to go?"

Down that hall, second door on the right."

Tattie smiled. "Then we'll deal with that skin damage you acquired over the summer. Once we are done, the pretty young girls will be fawning over you again."

"They never were, so any fawning will be an improvement. Will it be an immersive bath or skin cream this time?"

"A touch-up with cream…and you will love her fingers."

"Then let's get on with it. I have a busy day."

The same technician was there as last time, waiting for

me in his protective gear. We exchanged perfunctory greetings and I rolled up my sleeve and sat myself down on the lounger. Blood cleaning usually took two hours, hooked up to a machine that replaced blood plasma with fresh saline and albumin, plus what Doctor Tattie called our "special sauce" that consisted of a patented blend of biologicals tailored to my needs.

The tech hooked me up, one line in, one out, and in between a machine that pumped and monitored. It all looked rather primitive, the technology not having changed in decades. Despite the machine humming hypnotically beside me and the tech using his best calming presence, I usually found it hard to relax during these sessions, anxiety conflicting with boredom. It was like taking a sedative and a stimulant at the same time. But eventually I fell asleep only to be awoken by Doctor Tattie, shaking my shoulder, and saying, "Amir, your skin treatment is next. Please sign the invoice I sent. And oh…give my best regards to Darwina, will you?"

My mind spasmed fully awake. Darwina? What does she have to do with him? I hate these coincidences that often are not. "You…you know her?"

"Oh yes…rather well, in fact," he chuckled in a strangely suggestive way.

"But she is—" I stopped myself.

"She is living with you, isn't she?"

"Yes, yes…she—"

"Then please convey my fondest greetings. She will understand."

"Umm, alright." I said, my mind striving to unseize.

***

Later that day, Nora brought some cake to share. "You have the skin of a young girl," she grinned, licking icing off her fingers.

Her comment left me wondering if it was a compliment or criticism. "I...ahh...had a skin treatment. Looks like that for a few days. Doesn't last though. But it does remove any traces of skin cancer."

Nora finished the last of her licking and mumbled, "Uh huh."

"Apologies. Not an appetizing topic, is it?"

Her weak smile was followed by a swallow. It was one of those splendid late fall days, the air crisp, the light clear, the wildlife active, readying for winter. I gazed out the window trying to keep my eyes off Nora, but it was not easy. She was just so perfect, so like the one who yet lived in my heart.

"I'm glad you friended Neep," she said, breaking the awkward pause.

"Nosey little fellow."

"That's his job. Sorry he snooped through your home...searching for threats."

"Threats?"

"Yes, I hired him for security after that issue we had."

"Hmm. He looks more like a lapdog than a security dog."

"That's the point. Who would imagine? But he's over thirty and you wouldn't believe the tricks he knows."

"Like sit up and beg?"

Nora laughed. "He knows all those too. I was referring to security tricks. Electronics are not fully effective these days. A combo with biological is much better, or so I was advised.

Anyway, he is awfully expensive, so I assume he knows what he's doing."

"Expensive as in dog treats?" I said that hoping to elicit another of her lovely smiles. She did not disappoint.

"Hah! I wish. But now that he has your smell and is on your friend list, you are safe."

"Good to know I won't be throttled in bed by a terrier."

Nora smiled again then changed the subject, "Darwina told me you were married long ago."

"Yes...yes I was."

"You must be over it then."

"What do you mean?"

"There are no pictures nor momentos...that I can see, anyhow. Unless you have a secret room full of them, like those crazy people in the vids."

"It's what they recommended back then...to deal with grief."

"Oh. I'm sorry...didn't mean to imply."

"No worries."

Nora smiled. My heart ached, her smile so like my wife's. I still remembered her clearly. Years of therapy having had little effect.

"What are you thinking?" Nora asked.

"Nothing."

"We are always thinking. But I am prying. Sorry."

"It's not an easy subject."

"Your wife?"

"Yes."

"What happened to her?"

I had not discussed this in decades. But with Nora, I found

myself speaking, as if to my wife. I told her of how we met at a charity event, of our wedding at our friend's home, of my wife's career as a nurse while I was in graduate school, and of our dream to have a home and children.

"So sweet, a traditional love story," Nora said after I had paused.

"I suppose."

Nora's eyes flickered. "Must go," she said. "Have a designer on the way. You can tell me the rest later."

I watched her leave, feeling uneasy I had shared too much.

| 6 |

Chapter Six

It was past midnight when Darwina returned. "Where have you been?" I said in an unfortunate tone.

She flung her shoulder bag on the chair by the entrance. "You aren't my parent, Amir."

"And you didn't respond to my messages."

She shrugged, "I'm off to bed, if you're done with the interrogation."

"People worry, you know."

"People like you?"

"You could do worse."

"Alright, I'm sorry, Amir. Goodnight, then."

I nodded and watched her hang up her jacket. Then in the living room light, I noticed that her shirt was stained with dark blotches, her face scratched, and there was a red, swollen area by her left ear.

"What in hell happened to you?" I blurted.

"Oh Amir, you don't want to know."

"Does it involve me?"

"Maybe, but I'm too tired to discuss it now."

"Hmm. Alright, then. See you tomorrow."

She was on her way to the stairs that lead to her room in the basement when she stopped and turned back to me. "Please make sure all the doors and windows are locked. Goodnight, Amir...and thank you for caring."

**

"Oh, almost forgot, Doctor Tattie sends his regards," We were waiting for Nora to arrive. I watched Darwina's damaged face for the response.

She flinched, then replied casually, "Oh yes...we are old friends...sort-of."

"Old friends?"

"Yes, old friends, his younger sister and I are..." She crooked her finger in the direction of the hall bulletin board where Nora had stuck her note requesting sound absorbers on, etc.

I did so, only to hear a snuffling at my front door. We were ready for another meeting of our neighbourhood sex club where no one has sex. I opened the front door before it rang. Neep scooted between my legs and made directly for Darwina who lifted him for a doggy kiss.

"Sadly, we can't hear his opinions during our meeting since his implant is off. But he said he would growl if he disagreed and wag his tail if all was well," Nora explained as she took off her coat.

"Glad to know we'll have his wise input," I said.

Neep stared at me and gave a growl.

"You are being sarcastic. He hates that you know," Nora said, then settled in her favourite chair by the imitation fireplace.

"Darwina knows my ReGen doctor," I said to them both. "I need to know more. Mystery connections make me nervous. Surely you know that by now."

"What happened to your face?" Nora asked Darwina.

"Alright. Here goes. I'm taking a big risk here," Darwina proceeded to tell us that Doctor Allan Tattie is not only an old friend, but a member of her "action group", as she called it, a group dedicated to investigating conspiracies and righting wrongs. And that is how she got herself beaten up yesterday while asking questions about a church.

I interrupted. "Let me guess. Was it the Church of Infinite Love?"

Darwina touched her bruised cheek, "How did you know?"

"Remember I told you that political parties were banned? Well some went underground as religions or clubs that *are* legal."

"Social clubs and religions are free to meet...and organize," Nora mumbled. "Hmm, but why were you investigating that church?"

"Well, there are rumours, and more rumours, but one persistent one is that the Church of Infinite Love is the organization behind the burning of the library."

"What!" Nora exclaimed, almost levitating herself out of the chair.

"If so, they may have crossed the line with that one," I mused.

"People are upset. Some are evening willing to talk."

"And you got yourself punished for snooping," Nora said.

Neep whined. Three heads turned to him. He whined again.

"Security? You want us to discuss it?" Nora asked him. Neep wagged his tail and ran in a happy circle.

"Neep beefed up my home security, but Amir's is lacking. He made a list. It's in here somewhere." She dug through the pockets of her sweater till she found it. "Here, better do as my expert says."

"Most certainly, I will," I said, bowing to the little dog. "But all this is making me nervous. I need more security because my house mate is sticking her nose where she shouldn't? I thought we were done with this nonsense."

Darwina stiffened. "That's why I didn't want to tell you. I can leave if you don't have the guts to stand up for what is right."

Nora glared at her. "We mustn't fight. This isn't easy for any of us. Let's consider it carefully though. I believe Neep will keep us safe when we are at home. But then there are other places—"

"Yes, and how did you manage to get yourself mugged with all the surveillance everywhere?"

Darwina rolled her eyes, obviously annoyed with me. "It's *not* everywhere, is it? We even have maps of the Core with the surveillance dead spots clearly marked."

"So, you just happened to wander into a known dead spot?"

"I didn't wander, I knew the risks." Darwina banged her teacup on my priceless maple side table.

I did not want to antagonize her with more questions. The

four of us sat quietly, listening to the fake fire sizzle and the wind outside making the trees chatter.

"We are still friends," Nora said, "but do we want to go forward with this?"

"Perhaps, but in future we need to consult *before* we put each other's lives at risk," I said.

Four heads nodded in agreement.

Darwina smiled, leaned forward, and said, "Then this is what I suggest we do next."

***

I did not like it much, but it was a plan. Tattie had finagled an invite to join the church on a trial basis. There was a reception for new members this weekend coming, and he would be attending. The thing is that Darwina and Nora must stay far away from him, lest he be tainted. And messaging was out of the question, so it was up to me to handle communications, face-to-face, as I was his patient. It was logical until one remembered these may be the same people who burned the library, threatened Nora, and hacked the citizen assembly. What could go wrong?

"Get an appointment with Tattie before he goes. A mutual friend passed him a paper yesterday and he's expecting you to contact him. And be careful. Don't want him blown before the project begins," Darwina instructed me carefully like I was a schoolboy. We were walking in the nearby woods where people take their dogs and we had taken Neep for cover. He was acting like a proper dog for a change, but I knew he had sensors on in case we were being watched.

"I'll make something up to get an appointment. Just hope

his office isn't bugged. We'll need an excuse to turn off our AI's," I said, the worry jitters already starting.

"He'll make something up. He's good at that."

"At excuses?"

Darwina gave a questioning glance. "Didn't mean it that way. He's good...for a man. You can trust him."

"Hmm. Heard that one before."

"Not too late to back out Amir. But once you start—"

"It's just nerves, and I've been disappointed before."

Darwina smiled. "We'll pull you out if it gets sticky."

"Heard that one before too."

"I guess that's what happens when you live too long," Darwina chuckled then must've regretted her comment because she took my arm and said, "Sorry Amir."

"It only hurts because it may be true. We become like abused animals who flinch at the merest indication of trouble."

"Neep will protect us."

"Sure." I looked around and no Neep. "I think we lost our bodyguard."

"Neep! Come boy!" Darwina yelled.

Seconds later, he came scampering out of the woods, a cheerful look on his face and his little body fouled with muck. "Oh my! Nora will not be pleased," she said.

***

I met with Tattie later that day and we went over our amateur signals protocol. It was laughable, amounting to no more than a cipher, and the use of old-fashioned drop sites in public places where we could exchange messages between in-person meetings. We decided on the Iraqi café in St. George's

Square. Turns out Tattie lived nearby in one of those expensive apartments by the river.

"You just need a few minor adjustments to your meds," he said loud enough for everyone in the building to hear.

"Thank you, I hope it improves my hearing."

Tattie grinned. It was an amusing game. "It should and we can turn our AI's back on now. The tests are done."

I prayed the opposition were stupid, otherwise we were entering the forbidden zone. In for a penny, in for a pound, as we used to say. I was fully expecting a friendly visit from the police when I arrived home, but nothing happened. That was comforting and I told myself that I was as ready for this as my timid heart permitted.

***

Those few days went by all too slowly. Nora was busy imagineering, and Darwina had placed a trash bin out front of Nora's house and was filling it with the debris she had thrown off the roof. Neep was ever watchful, prowling the neighbourhood as they worked. It was quiet. Too quiet, as they say. But I knew it was just my mind. Our neighbourhood always was quiet.

Each day I would go to the square and have my coffee, then use the washroom. The stall on the end was where we had agreed to hide our messages, in the toilet tank, using waterproof paper carefully folded and stuck to the side above the waterline. I had told them of the book cipher employed during the Cold War. We used identical copies of the Revised Standard Version of the Bible, New Testament, assigning a string of numbers for book, chapter, verse, and word number. For example, book one is Matthew, chapter two starts with "Now when Jesus...", verse five in chapter two starts with "They told him...", and word number three is "him". The resulting code for the word "him" was 1,2,5,3. For this to work properly we had to use the same version of the Bible. I already had mine and I prayed Tattie could find one online to buy. It was not an easy code to break, even with the best decryption.

There were two flaws with this method. The first being that it took a lot of time coding and decoding messages. Darwina had suggested using a searchable online version of the Bible. But if anyone discovered Tattie and I were searching the same book, we were done. Best to use paper books in a place with no security cameras. The second problem was that we had to physically go to the same place to exchange messages. No way around that, and if one of us was being tracked and a pattern emerged and we were flagged, we were done. There was no perfect system. We just had to hope we could get away with it for awhile, until we answered the questions we had about the church.

***

It is infuriating how slow time goes by when one is waiting. But Saturday came and went with no news from Tattie. I had been dutifully visiting the café toilet each day, but no luck and I did not want to risk contacting him in case someone was watching. It was all up to him now. The rest of us were increasingly on edge, including Mr. Neep who was sleeping less and prowling more. The worst of it was we could not even discuss it without setting up a sex club meeting, and too many of those would set off alarms somewhere. So, we waited and fretted.

It came on Monday, the note, folded and stuck to the inside of the toilet tank. I raced home for my Bible and within minutes it was deciphered: "In trial done". I called an emergency sex club meeting for that evening.

***

"Clear as pea soup," said Darwina after we had read and re-read the message several times, as if that would help.

"Could he not have used more words?" Nora asked, as perplexed as she looked.

"Sounds like a telegram," I added, forgetting they likely had no idea what that mean. By the quizzical looks that followed, I had to add, "Telegrams were how they used to send messages last century. You had to pay by the word, and it was expensive, so people were economical with the words. It was an art to write a good telegram with few words and clear meaning."

"Sounds like those stupid text messages from the early days of the internet too," Nora said.

"Sort of. But that doesn't help us. What *does* our message mean?" I wondered aloud.

"OK. Let's assume it is like an old text or telegram. It could mean Tattie is in a trial that is done." Darwina wrote that down on paper.

"Or how about that he is in and the trial is done?" Nora said, Darwina adding it to the list.

"But what does he mean by "in"? In what? In trouble...in the church...in his office...in trial?"

Darwina threw her pencil, across the room. "This is

pointless. We are just guessing. There's no way around it, we need a face meeting."

Their eyes swivelled to me. I sighed. "Alright, but I just saw him last week, and my coverage—"

Nora gave me one of those smiles. "Amir, we have no choice, unless you want to pass more confusing messages back and forth, and Tattie has never done this before."

"I guess I'll have to make up some reason," I said. I think she was beginning to understand my weakness.

***

I pretended to have a sore leg to get my appointment. Of course, it was silly because the ReGen treatments pretty much precluded sore body parts unless one was very imprudent. Even the receptionist must have thought I looked ridiculous as he was hiding a smirk behind his gaily painted hand. But at least it got me in, but I had to be careful from now on, being maxed out on my coverage for the month.

"You look well, Amir," Tattie said, sarcastically mimicking the receptionist's face.

"Not sure the drugs are working. Feel old as hell this week…aching all over," I answered, silently mouthing that we needed privacy.

But strangely he seemed not to understand and asked about my aches and pains. I answered with a flailing of arms and exaggerated miming he did not seem to comprehend. So, I grabbed a note tablet from his desk and wrote, "Church. What happened?"

His eyes blinked. His grin inverted. He cleared his throat, "Don't know why you are being so cryptic, Amir. Do you mean the church I joined last weekend? I guess I must've mentioned it last time."

I nodded vigorously and shrugged in that gesture of not understanding.

"Oh, you want to know how it went? Ahh. Are the drugs making you mute? Never seen that side-effect before."

I sighed.

Tattie consulted his AI reference. "Nope, you must be the first. I will enter it in the database. Hmm."

I sighed very loudly and pointed to the tablet again.

"Ahh. You want to know what happened?"

I nodded so wildly it made him chuckle.

"You are in quite a state, aren't you? Well, if you must know I absolutely *love* my new church with *all* my new friends. They do a lot of charity work in the community."

Oh gosh, I thought. *Something is terribly wrong.*

I listened while he babbled on about the delightful food they served and the friendly meeting he had with the church elders.

"Umm doctor, I think I might be fine if I reduce the dose for a while. It may just be that it is *evolving*, somehow," I said, hoping that word would remind him of Darwina.

"Oh, you *can* speak. Wonderful! Yes, you can halve the dosage for a week. It won't matter much in the long run."

Then it occurred to me that he knew he was being watched, and that explained why he could not turn off AI's, and why he was acting like this. "I'll do that. Meanwhile, I need to have a good coffee at my favourite place, and likely use the washroom and flush the toilet thereafter."

He tilted his head sideways like a dog. "As you wish Amir. Have a delightful day and enjoy your coffee. I am afraid my next patient is waiting."

I said my goodbyes and slouched out of his office not knowing what exactly had happened. It had been worse than sending secret Bible messages.

***

I could not even mention my meeting with Tattie without calling a special meeting. So, to kill time I went to the Square and my favourite café. It was one of those brilliant fall days with tree leaves colouring the sky and chrysanthemums glorious in their planters. It reminded me of when my parents emigrated from Iraq, and when they complained of the cold and were informed that winter had yet to begin. Despite their constant discomfort and grumbling, they stayed for my sake.

Soon it would be the transition from fall to winter and all that entails, including much consumption and even more traditional joy, in service of another futile attempt to ward-off winter's coming depression. For me, it was just another reminder that I had no family left alive. It was that sad thought which accompanied me to the café washroom where I hoped to find a note from Tattie that explained what really had happened at his church meeting.

The toilet was faux Victorian with gleaming white porcelain, brass fittings, imitation wood paneling, and an embossed metal ceiling. It had two completely enclosed metal stalls with secure locks and electronic vacancy indicators on each door. My target was the toilet tank mounted on the wall above the toilet bowl. I was reaching for it when I heard the washroom door open followed by a sniffle and sneeze. Next, whoever it was tried my door. I thought that odd since I knew the stall next to me was vacant and mine clearly occupied and locked. I said nothing. The person left immediately.

I fished around in the tank. No note. I wiped my wet hand on my trousers and turned to leave then hesitated a moment thinking of that odd behaviour with my door. I shook the paranoia away and pushed the pad on the stall door to leave.

The shock I received was hard to describe. And I mean a real shock, not a metaphorical one. It was electric and strong and left me on me on my ass on the floor, vibrating and barely holding back puke. I stilled myself before calling for help. Eventually an attendant came. He was duly apologetic. Then as he was helping me leave, he wondered aloud what that lump was attached to the outside of my stall door. He reached for it. I pulled his hand back and said, "Better call the police."

***

"What do you think it was?" Darwina said as soon as we had started our secure sex club meeting that evening.

"A message," I replied.

She nodded.

"Could've been worse," Nora added. "At least you are alive."

"There is that…" I agreed.

"You should've remembered that public washrooms have no cameras. They are indicated on my dead spot map. You should've taken a map," Darwina chided.

"That's precisely why I put the drop there," I countered.

"Matters not. We can no longer use that place. Now tell us again about Tattie in case we missed anything." Nora took charge of the questioning and we went over it all one more time. I was still suffering the twitches, my mind almost use-less for clear thought. I had to depend on my friends for this one. Darwina looked like a gamin assassin in her lab-grown brown leather and olive drab synth suit, her tawny face tight with anger. Neep seemed un-interested, except in the plush toy he was shaking as though a rat. And Nora, always beauti-ful even when head-sunk like an owl in her sweater.

Darwina concluded, "Don't think he met his soul mates at that church meeting. Something else happened to him."

"Or he was playing along because he knew someone was listening," Nora suggested.

"But how did they know about the toilet?" I asked for about the third time.

"Obvious. Either Tattie told them, or you were followed."

Neep threw up a wad of drool-coated toy stuffing on my antique Iraqi rug, then let out a loud yap.

"I think he agrees," Darwina giggled.

I retrieved a wipe while they went over what to do next. Then it occurred to me. "Nora, is it possible to brainwash or control people through their thought messaging and AI im-plants?"

Nora's neck extended like a turtle out of its shell. Neep barked. Darwina gurgled what sounded like a curse. "I was consulting the AI on that very topic. It said no. Built-in safe-guards, and so on. But would an AI always tell the truth? Would it admit to messing with our minds?"

I shifted uncomfortably in my chair. "We need to be care-ful with this. Paranoia is a bunny hole we don't want to en-ter."

"Still…" Nora said, sinking back in her sweater.

"Well, is it possible, Nora?" I asked again.

Nora nodded slowly. "Not tight control, perhaps more like suggestions and positive reinforcement. But yes, it is possible, but very illegal. AI's are supposed to be impartial."

"How might that work? How could Tattie have been turned?" I asked.

"Simple. Find out as much about him as you can and exploit weakness. Feed him praise at the right time on specific subjects. Offer calculated inducements. Here's an example. Let's assume they find out Tattie is insecure about his work. Maybe he is not the most brilliant of ReGen doctors. Maybe he has been disciplined. Yet he loves the work and will do anything to keep his job and status, and of course the credits that allow him to live well. Then imagine what you can do with this information. Control feeding his desires and you can control him. None of this is new, of course, just enabled efficiently with AI's and thought messaging. It's extremely hard to keep secrets from those who have access. Even our innermost desires are played out daily in subtle ways. For example, Amir, you like your Iraqi café, yet haven't been to Iraq since you were a child, right? It's likely you long to return or miss your family and culture. Is that not so?"

"As easy as that?" Darwina asked. "Can't imagine what they have on me."

"So, you think Tattie is being played?" I asked for clarification.

"Maybe. Could be the thought messaging and AI are being used somehow to influence him," Nora replied.

"But would he suspect he's being manipulated?" I asked.

Nora considered it a moment before answering. "Not necessarily. It's our unconscious mind that decides, in most cases, then informs our consciousness. Conscious decision is largely an illusion, although the conscious mind can over-rule the unconscious."

"And it may be hard to tell which is which," I added.

"I don't believe any of this. Tattie's no fool. Must be more than suggestions affecting the unconscious mind. In any case, he needs an intervention before it's too late." Darwina was half-way out the door before we knew it.

"Do nothing foolish, Darwina!" I yelled after her. "Remember your pledge. Consult us first."

The door slammed. Nora closed her eyes and sunk deeper into her sweater. Neep folded his paws over his eyes. I wanted to disappear too.

***

The Basilica of Our Lady Immaculate is in the Core on what used to be called Catholic Hill. Darwina was right. Tattie needed help. And the best way to lure him without setting off warning sirens everywhere was for his sister Rebecca to invite him to Mass. There were few things sacrosanct these days, but they included freedom of religious practice, within bounds, of course.

I never quite understood the hold religion had on people, especially Christianity, although Jesus seemed a good sort. The religions these days taught that they all come from God. Strange considering many of the teachings conflict. *Maybe God is so old, she has memory problems*, I thought, then immediately asked for forgiveness. But whatever. The differences were acceptable provided we did not fight over them, as we did not many generations ago. In the end, it was the political system which was sacrificed in the name of peace. But too, the religions had been warned to play nice or they would be next for the chopping block. That was the gist of it anyway, and so far, it had worked, and religion had made a strong comeback.

We were near the back pews since the building mostly was filled by the time we arrived. It was a regular Sunday Mass; Rebecca had told us before we entered. She was one of those plump and plain ever smiling women, who would not look out of place in a farmer's market selling vegetables. When I asked her what she did, she replied, "I knit...from wool."

Close enough, I thought.

Our happy knitter sat primly beside her brother while he focused his attention on the stunning stained-glass windows in the nave. I was wedged between him and Darwina, with Nora on her other side. Our plan was to lure Tattie into the basement of the basilica after Mass. There is an un-used door behind a cabinet down there. The door leads to a tunnel that goes to the tavern across the street. "If you don't believe me, have a look in the library archives," I had told them. "Oh wait. The archives are gone," I added as a joke no one found humorous. But they were astonished, especially when I told them how the tunnel had been used. Assuming we could get Tattie into the tunnel, we could have a proper chat free from the ever-present ears of our minders. That is what we planned, anyway.

The service was pleasingly short. I was expecting hours,

but it was more like one, followed by a line-up for the faithful to eat a cracker and have a sip of wine. That gave me time to inspect the interior more carefully. It was quite delightful in its swooping vaults and curved windows with dark wood accents. I liked the whiteness of it all, as though God had swept it clean of defilement. Rebecca mentioned that we could visit during the week for a tour. I told her to sign me up after Nora had suggested we visit as a group.

"There is an elevator behind the altar in the hallway. I think it's called the ambulatory. The elevator is unlocked during Mass...for the disabled. We may be able to use it if we are careful," I explained, remembering what I'd been told by the old parson years ago when we had worked on a service project.

I had expected vigorous questioning by the others, but there was none. There were no other good options. We could not just kidnap Tattie in the open, could we? It had to be somewhere he normally would go that had a security dead zone. The only place we could think of was his church and the tunnel under it.

"Let's go light some candles behind the altar. Less people there," Rebecca whispered to her brother, taking his hand. We made our way slowly forward along the left aisle, smiling and nodding as we went. I brought my walking stick and pretend limp, and people thoughtfully made way as they saw me pass. I felt like a fraud, and worse, before God.

"Did you know there is a Holy Shrine in the basement," Rebecca said after they had lit their candles and tapped some credits.

"No, I didn't. Whose?" Tattie asked.

"Umm. I think Saint Al," she answered, looking to me for help.

"Why don't we go look. Could be a surprise," I said. "I think this elevator goes to it."

There were many people about, but no one questioned us as I limped my way into the elevator and motioned for the rest to follow. This was the tricky part: getting below and into the tunnel without being stopped. It was dodgy business and required more confidence than I currently possessed after having been zapped recently by the opposition. So, I let Nora steady my elbow as though I were a decrepit senior. Darwina lead with Tattie and Rebecca in tow.

"This way," I whispered, thanking providence there was no one in the basement to challenge us. There, the cabinet stood on the side wall. "We have to move this a bit. There should be a door behind it."

It was large and of carved wood but slid easily on the stone floor. The door behind it was small, as though built for the wee ones of legend. It was no more than five feet high with a rusted iron hasp and padlock. We stared at it. It did not stare back. In fact, it seemed to put a complete stop to our expedition. "Damn," I whispered.

Darwina grabbed the lock and tugged. "The screws seem loose," she muttered.

"Let's not break anything," Tattie whispered.

Darwina obviously did not agree because she yanked the lock several times, pulling the screws out of the wood. "The wood's rotten," she said, grinning.

The door creaked open just enough for each of us to squeeze through. Darwina was first in and ready with her finger light, but what greeted us was not pleasant. The scene was strait from a horror vid with a staircase leading down to dank blackness through a layered mass of spider webs.

"Not to worry, no lethal bugs in Guelph," Darwina said, pointing her light for me to clear a path through the webs with my stick.

I heard Tattie whisper to Rebecca, "Can we not do this some other time? They have a tour, and—"

"We are here and it's not much further," Rebecca cut in. Tattie sighed.

Darwina lead the way down. I followed close behind, batting bugs and webs out of the way, praying the stairs were not as rotted as the door. Thankfully, they creaked reassuringly with no sudden cracks or snaps. I told everyone to hang on the rail for safety. They scoffed. Darwina countermanded that with the suggestion we go slow and watch our footing since the railing was home to who knows what critters. The stairs took us about ten feet down to a small landing. The spider webs diminished but the air smelled of sewer and we could hear water running nearby.

"This way," I said, dimly seeing the opening on the far wall. "There should be a spring up ahead where the tunnel widens."

"Strange place to put a shrine. Who'd want to come down here?" Tattie grumbled.

We shuffled along. I held onto Darwina's belt lest she fall in a hole, her finger light proving barely adequate for the task. The tunnel sloped down the hill, the damp walls oppressively close. At least there were no more spiders, just unknown shapes which moved on the walls and floors, or perhaps they were tricks of light. I did not want to stop and find out. We continued in silence enduring private fears. The sound of the water grew louder. I told Darwina to watch for it. Did not want her falling in and I had no idea where it might lead.

"That must be it," she whispered, pointing to a reflection ahead. The tunnel widened into a small cavern about twelve feet in diameter. Along one wall was the spring, sheeting down the wall into a jumble of rocks then disappearing below.

"It collapsed years ago and filled the pool." I consulted my AI for more. It was dead. "We should be safe now. We're at least fifteen feet below the surface. No signals down here."

"Eh?" said Tattie as he and Rebecca joined us in the middle of the cavern.

"Dear brother, listen to me," Rebecca started.

Tattie swung around to look "Don't see the shrine."

Rebecca took his arm, stopping him. "Please forgive us, the shrine was a ruse to rescue you."

I quietly repositioned myself to catch him in case he decided to flee back up the tunnel. Darwina and Nora did the same on both sides.

"Eh?" Tattie said again, sounding confused.

Rebecca moved closer. "We are worried about you, and we need to talk in private."

"There's no shrine? Then why—"

"Brother you joined that church, and we need to know why. The beautiful basilica above is our church. Our family helped build it. Why did you leave us? Why?"

Tattie shook his head, as though trying to remove water from his ear.

"What? I don't know. I didn't..."

Rebecca continued, "Our friends have concerns about your new church...about its political activities—"

"What! No! They are nice...they are..." Tattie's head turned to and froe. "No, no!"

I had worried he would run, instead he started to sob. We closed in, surrounding him with hugs, his sister whispering that it was OK, all will be well and that she loved him. In a while he calmed. "I don't understand. I felt guided, loved...for the first time...accepted."

"You have always been loved and accepted by me, dear Allan."

"I think they got in your head Tattie," Darwina said, perhaps too coldly. "Now we have to get them out."

Nora spoke next, "We need to find out who can do this, and we need to stop them. We're sunk if they can mentally kidnap us. Tattie's safe down here. But once we go back, they could reassert control."

"Agreed, but we also need to know what happened to him at that church meeting. It might give is some clues about how they did it," Darwina added.

Tattie was exceptionally good at recalling. He told us that the service was religious and friendly. Then came the private meeting with the church elders. "I was seated in a chair set before them. I think the chair was metal with little knobbly things on the back support, like one of those massage chairs. I felt a calming sensation almost immediately. Behind the wooden table in front of me sat four elders, all men, wearing black suits and white ties. They were very welcoming and smiling and asked me about my life and why I wanted to join.

It was all quite normal but for that chair which seemed to pulse when I gave my answers. The questioning was over in several minutes. Then the attendant who'd brought me came to help me out of the chair. I'm glad he did because my legs were wobbly. I could hardly walk at first. Next day I was informed I'd been accepted."

"Please describe that chair again," Nora asked.

"Nothing much to describe. They said it was to calm people because they know those interviews can be stressful. I thought it very considerate of them."

"Did you feel a prick or sting in your back?" Nora asked.

"Umm...no, not that I remember."

I could see where Nora was going with this, "Tattie, do you mind if we have a look at your back? Just in case...you know."

Rebecca nodded, "Please lift your shirt Allan, so we can check."

He was reluctant but complied. Darwina focused her finger light on him. The three of us looked closely. I saw nothing.

"Maybe there?" Nora pointed. "That hair doesn't look right...different colour. Hard to know what it is without a signal scan. It's close to his spinal cord too."

Darwina retrieved a pen and made a circle on his skin around the area.

"I have a meter at home, but we can't discuss it openly there," Nora noted.

"If they have implanted something, we'll get it out or break it," Darwina promised.

"And we have to do this quickly before they regain control once we go above," I said.

"It won't be enough to deal with whatever it is in his back," Nora said, looking ghoulishly white.

"I know, we must also find out who is behind it," I said.

Nora nodded, "Especially the techs. Are they local, or from away? We need to neutralize them, or we have no chance."

Darwina pointed her finger light at Tattie. "I think we need one more foray into that church next Sunday."

"At this point we don't know if the church leaders are behind this, or a rogue group operating from within," Nora said.

"And he may be walking into a trap if they know his implant isn't working," I said, thinking how fast these things can go badly.

"He's our only way in," Darwina countered "Or we can remove the implant, call it a day and let them win."

There was silence for a moment as we considered alternatives.

"Brother, are you up for this? They may have control of your mind. Understand?"

Tattie nodded, then muttered, "Damn them to hell. Get that thing out of me. And I *will* go back to their church to find out who did this to me. I'm not afraid of them."

"Umm," I muttered, then thought the better of advising caution again. Tattie truly was our only chance and we had to take it. "Settled. Now, let's get out of here before someone notices."

We made our way carefully back to the staircase, my mind

weighted with anxieties of what might come. The shuffling sound of our feet was broken by Darwina's voice, "I kind of like it down here. Is there another entrance so I don't have to use that creepy basilica?"

"Yes. This tunnel ends in the tavern cellar. They used to make beer there and created the tunnel to access spring water."

"Ahh...I must look. This would be an excellent hiding place."

"There's a boarded-up door in the tavern, or so I've heard. And another tunnel that exits behind the church which was used by bootleggers. Rumour has it Al Capone, the famous gangster, visited the tavern with his mistress."

"What fun! You must tell me more."

I chuckled, "Guelph is riddled with underground tunnels. Some legal, some not."

"Then I must explore."

"Yes, they would be a good place for a brat like you. You could join the rats, racoons and other vagrants."

"That's cruel, Amir. Darwina is no longer a vagrant. She has us," Nora laughed.

The joking that followed helped us to the staircase and there were four great sighs of relief when we emerged into the light and land of surveillance.

"Let's go home for lunch," I said, trying to sound as innocuous as possible.

***

We had finished our quick tour of Nora's wreck of a home. She and Neep had shown us the security system they installed, including a button-board on the floor Neep could operate with his nose. But we were here for Tattie and Neep smelled that spot Darwina had circled at the base of Tattie's back that made Nora's meter glow. Neep confirmed with a growl. Dog and electronics in agreement, Nora nodded and placed her meter aside. Now we had to decide what to do. Remove it and prove we knew what they were doing or try to damage it and hope they would fall for Tattie's excuse. We chose the latter and had to be careful we said nothing suspicious in the process.

"Nora, what will you do with this room?" I asked, already knowing the answer.

"It will be my new dining room. Come look at the new electronic controls they are installing."

"Fascinating, isn't it, Tattie? You might want one of these for your home," I said.

"Careful you two, there might be live wires over there," cautioned Darwina, setting up what was to come next. Darwina had rigged some wires to an old battery she had salvaged from the snowblower. Tattie lifted his shirt and turned his back to her then closed his eyes. I was positioned on one side of him and Nora on the other.

"Makes me nervous. You two shouldn't be messing with that," Rebecca chimed in.

"No worries, just having a look," I said, then nodded to Darwina who immediately plunged the wires into his back.

"Gaaa!" Tattie shouted, not faking it.

Darwina removed the wires and stepped out of the way before he fell on her. We grabbed him in time and laid him gently on the floor, his body trembling, a sheen of sweat glistening his face.

"Brother, what happened?" Rebecca yelled, following the script.

"I think he must have touched something," Nora said. "Are you OK, Tattie?"

"Y...yes...help...me up, please."

Meanwhile Neep was running in circles barking, a gleeful look on his furry face. The play must be going well. Then he ran over and sniffed Tattie's back again and announced with another happy bark that all was well. Nora silently mouthed that her meter indicated it was dead. We knelt beside Tattie. Rebecca started to sob. I wondered how this foolery could possibly end well.

| 7 |

Chapter Seven

Our nerves were frayed all that week since we were expecting repercussions from our escapade in the tunnel and the destruction of Tattie's implant. We decided it was some form of remote acupuncture device that could stimulate his pleasure centers. At least that technology was possible, according to Nora, who was becoming increasingly obsessed with discovering who could deploy all this illegal tech without the authorities noticing. It was indeed a puzzle, but my focus was more on the level of self-preservation, so I insisted we take it one step at a time and regularly re-evaluate our risk profile, as we had been taught in government to prevent embarrassing of our masters.

"We may be able to use these bikes on Sunday," Darwina said, holding one by the handlebar.

"They need the tires pumped, chain oiled, and a run around the block to make sure they work," I added.

Tattie was determined to go on Sunday, and he needed backup. So, we decided it would be Darwina and I on old bikes, using the trail that wound through the area by the church.

"Then let's get them out of the basement, just in case they don't work," Darwina said, her fingers already blackened with oil. She relished the idea of tinkering with them, so I left her to it.

***

Our plan was fraught with potential failure. Tattie would go in alone, attend the service, ask sensitive questions, try to eavesdrop on private meetings, and get out alive. Meanwhile, his backup consisted of a hotheaded brat and an ancient codger with no weapons and on primitive bicycles sans power assist. But that is how it stood when Sunday morning rolled around. At least the bikes worked, and it was not pouring rain when we set out.

I enjoyed the ride more than expected, making a mental note to get out like this more often. Our plan was to ensure Tattie left the church by twelve noon at the latest and we had chosen a spot on the trail where we could see the main door clearly. Tattie arrived on schedule having used the minibus that served the area. He glanced back at us and smiled. Darwina sighed and slapped her forehead. I turned my suit warmer to medium for the wait.

We said little to each other in the hour or so we stood on the trail, pretending to consult our bike computers and sip water for the benefit of any security cameras pointed in our direction. Several people passed us on their bikes, as well as runners and dog walkers. It was a busy place on a Sunday. We were lucky. They were good cover. "We should do this more often," Darwina said, chewing her fingernail out of nervous boredom.

"There are other trails, too. The ones along the river are better."

"Then it's a date."

"A date."

"And maybe Nora has a bike." Darwina grinned.

I winked at her. "I'll find her one."

"I'm sure—"

Suddenly, the side door of the church flew open, followed by Tattie walking quickly in our direction, his face already inflamed and chest puffing from exertion.

"Oh, oh. Get ready," Darwina whispered.

Two large men exited the church next. They looked fit and fast but were confused before they spotted Tattie entering the woods near us. They flew after him. We panicked.

"Here Tattie! Get on my bike!" Darwina yelled.

Tattie struggled to mount even with Darwina helping him. I jumped off my bike and we were able to get him rolling down the trail with us pushing. "Pedal!" Darwina yelled after him. But it was too late for us. To escape, we planned to ride my bike in tandem, with Darwina on the cross bar. But they would be on us before we could manage that. I turned to confront them, but Darwina grabbed my hand and shouted, "Not here, run!"

I followed her into the brush beside the trail. It led down to a marsh. The men were right behind us, grunting and speaking a foreign tongue. Darwina pushed her way through the cattails, slowing as the mud sucked her boots. I could see water ahead. "Can you swim?" she asked.

"Yes, but—" I was about to say, "but not in a swamp," however too late because she dove forward and started stroking her way through the remaining plants and into deeper water. I swore and followed her, the big man behind me grappling with my thrashing legs until I kicked backward and connected. That released him and I was able to swim free. It was not easy swimming wearing a jacket filled with water that wanted to hold me in place. But I was in open water, the adrenaline pushing me onward, my heart rate monitor pegged at max, my stupid AI telling me to stop and meditate. Panic quickly changed to cold. Strange how the mind can only deal with one overriding sensation at a time.

Darwina was treading water ahead. "We need to get out of here before we freeze," she yelled, as though I needed to be told. "I think there's a trail on the other side. Let's go."

It was no more than fifty meters, but it may as well have been a kilometer. I almost drowned. But I said nothing to her. Did not want her coming back to save a codger. Wouldn't be fair. Fortunately, the pond shallowed before the shore and my feet touched bottom in time. She pulled me out with a yip and a shout about it being great fun. For me it was another horrific experience I would have to forget with the help of drugs and counselling.

Darwina removed my jacket and wrung it out while I squeezed the water out of my suit. "I think if we go that way, the trails join, and we can walk to the minibus stop," she pointed in the direction she intended.

I was beginning to shiver. "My suit warmer must've failed."

"You didn't wear the all-weather one?"

"Didn't expect to go swimming. Did you?"

"I was ready for anything," she grinned. "Let's get you home before you catch a chill."

"Well, we agree on that at least."

"I hope Tattie can find his way home. He was going the wrong way last we saw him."

Then it occurred to me. "We need to contact Rebecca. Tattie can't go home, can he?"

"Oh gosh, you're right. Can you run? I'll order a car and contact her."

The nice fast run was what I needed, and I was feeling better by the time we reached the car stop.

Later we learned that Rebecca was waiting for Tattie when he arrived at her home hours later. That was a particularly good thing, including the fact that he had obtained pertinent names and conversations. Rebecca then escorted her brother to the only secure place she could think of: Nora's home with Neep and his web of dog security.

It was supper time, and we were desperately hungry and tired. We agreed to meet next day to discuss what had been found.

***

Some believe I am cynical, but they are quite wrong. It is just that I have lived an exceedingly long time and through observation have come to believe that life mostly unfolds because of cause and effect. It could be karma, but I am not sure it is psychic. I prefer to think of it as a law of nature, like gravity. So, I was not especially surprised to hear frantic banging on my front door in the middle of that night.

"Someone is in my house!" Nora screamed after slamming

and locking the door behind her. "Neep is fighting him! You must help!"

"Alright, alright," I said taking her by the elbow to her favourite chair by the fireplace.

Darwina joined us, having not bothered to dress properly. "What's the matter? What's going on?" she shouted in Nora's face, adding to the hysteria.

I quickly grabbed Darwina's coat from the hall closet and threw it at her.

Nora sobbed. "Neep had him by the leg and was shaking it like a rat..."

"Who?" I asked. "Who was *he*?"

"He's big...I think...and cursing like a man. He was swinging his leg trying to remove Neep. I'm so worried Neep will be hurt. It's all my fault. I should never—"

"What about Tattie?" I asked.

"He went to the basement to sleep...didn't see him after that," Nora answered.

Darwina did not wait for more explanation. She slipped on the jacket and grabbed the hockey stick she kept in the closet. "I'm going to find out," I heard her shout over her shoulder.

"No wait! This could be dangerous," I said, but my words proved futile.

"Oh damn!" I said. I was in robe and slippers, not very practical garb for taking on someone in the dark. But I could not leave it to Darwina, so I cinched my robe, grabbed the emergency light, and followed her.

At least Nora's house lights were working but the entry

way was even more of a disaster than usual. The living room looked like a bomb had gone off, with everything that should have been upright, not, and parts of the freshly finished drywall spattered with blood. And there, proudly panting amid the wreckage was little Neep, his nuzzle stained with blood. "Taught that guy a lesson," he thought proudly in my implant, his tongue flopping about wildly.

Darwina knelt beside him. "Is he still here?"

"No, he ran. Police are coming," Neep explained.

Nora joined us, wrapped in my coat she put on over her nightdress. She was a shaken and stirred mess, quite unlike her normally composed self. Nora sniffled and carefully walked through the broken materials to Neep. "I am so sorry, Neep. Are you OK?"

Neep held up his paw. "Broke a toenail and I can't lick because they need the blood on my whiskers. Forensics will find him."

"Oh, poor boy," Nora sobbed. "This is my fault. All my fault."

We had to be careful what we said because AI's were on, but I could not help taunting whoever might be listening in, "This could be a simple robbery, but if it is more nefarious, to the Devil may they go."

While we were gawking, Darwina went from room-to-room, her hockey stick at the ready. "Clear!" she shouted from the second floor.

"Better check the basement too and find Tattie," I told her.

"Bad man is gone. Tattie sleeping," Neep said.

Darwina returned a few minutes later. "Tattie is safe and on his way. Slept through it all."

"Geesh, wish I could sleep like that," I said.

"Try ear plugs. Worked for him. It's not safe for anyone here. That window is broken, and the back-door lock is ruined. You'll freeze if nothing else," Darwina said.

"Agreed. I have spare bedrooms you are welcome to use."

"I don't want this violence brought to your door," Nora replied. "I can get a hotel."

Darwina grabbed Nora by the sleeve. "Nonsense, we are safer together. I will take the first watch. Let's grab your clothes for tomorrow."

The cop bot arrived as we were waiting for Nora and Tattie. It asked in its perfectly calm voice what had happened. Thankfully, Neep took charge since they seemed to know each other professionally. A few minutes later the bot was on its way after having taken blood samples from Neep's face.

"DNA here matched one from a café at St. George's Square," Neep said, his face pensive.

"Ahh...the sneeze," I muttered, recalling the washroom.

Neep stared at me for a few seconds before continuing, "DNA not in regional database."

"Why am I not surprised," I said.

Neep tilted his head. "Cops will sequence it, get good description, send to international cops."

"And we could be dead before that gets back," I sighed. "When they introduced voluntary DNA sampling the main objection was that it would only be the good citizens who would cooperate, just like the gun issue of the previous generations." That pointless tirade off my chest, I grabbed a broom and started sweeping up the broken glass.

"Dead? Who is dead?" Tattie had just arrived and caught the tail end of my angst.

"No one yet. But you know how I am." I offered him the broom, but he turned away and mumbled something about a holy mess.

Nora arrived next, dressed in an outfit made for a safari. "Ooh, very nice," said Darwina, smiling.

"Just got it last week. Shape and texture change. More than one thousand combinations."

"Might smell after a few of those combos," I said.

"In fact, it won't. Self cleaning and made of bamboo with shape patterns and textures imbedded.

"Well, I hope it's warm."

"It can be warm or cool as desired," Darwina explained. "The latest ones even have outerwear included."

"Yes, mine does. It's in the menu, and—"

I left them discussing the exciting features of her new outfit to work on my pile of broken glass. A few minutes later, after having exhausted their fashion parley, Nora passed me heading for the door, saying, "Lets go. This place is giving me the creepies."

Neep evidently agreed because he scooted through her legs and was first out, asking if we had any tasty bits of food at home.

***

Next morning, I felt worse after a night of tossing, turning, and worrying what the future might bring. Before we went back to bed, Tattie said he would tell all, but we replied it would have to wait till next evening when we could convene our sex club. A formal invite was made which pleased Tattie greatly until I passed him a thought that explained sex meant no sex.

Nevertheless, no thugs came around that day to disturb our peace. We spent the time quietly licking our wounds and staying offline. The wee dog awoke with a limp too, evidently the result of being slammed against some hard things while he was being swung about by the perpetrator. However, his tail was wagging as he plotted revenge.

I was almost as bad off as Neep since I must have wrenched my shoulder when I was frantically thrashing about in the water. And I had a good laugh on receiving a cautionary message that my ReGen warrantee was under review because of the abuse my body had endured in recent months. I duly apologized and promised to be a good boy in future. The women seemed to have recovered faster than us guys since they were giggling about our adventures over breakfast.

"You look glum," Darwina said, grinning over their shared joke.

"Sore arm, sore shoulder, water in my ears, my ReGen coverage under threat, and I lost my bike. Can you blame me?" I answered.

"We were just discussing your bike," Darwina said. "Nora thinks we should retrieve it and have a look at that lovely neighbourhood too."

I set myself down at the breakfast table. "Umm, maybe some other day."

"It's a fine day. Nora and I will go in a car and see if we can find it. If not, at least we'll have a nice trail walk."

I looked at them both skeptically. Had they not met their

fill of danger? "The bike is old and worthless. Someone likely has it by now."

"We'll go anyway," Nora confirmed in a tone that meant it had been decided and please butt out.

I shrugged. "Have a good time then. Neep and I will use our time profitably." By that I meant moving his security system over here and setting it up, since we decided last night that Nora and Tattie would not be going back to her house till our situation was resolved. Seemed logical, but on going to bed the implications of that decision occupied my mind and was the main reason for my fitful sleep. The opposition clearly knew Tattie was here along with us troublemakers. It was only a matter of time before they struck again. And fearsome Neep was injured, his equipment damaged, and we had nothing more than a hockey stick and some kitchen knives to defend ourselves. We could go to the police, but chances are they could do nothing based on our unprovable allegations. All they had so far was blood and a DNA sample from someone not in their database. If it were up to me alone, I would leave town for a long vacation.

Tattie eventually pupated from the cocoon he had made in my spare bedroom. He looked good as new and apparently had cleansed his mind of yesterday's escape and the dangers confronting us. I watched him toddle off to the minibus station, humming a cheerful tune. That left Neep who was pestering me with requests for a chat. "No dog food here? And how about a bowl of clean water? I need to poop." It was like that, a constant string of demands for service. The water and letting him out were easy enough but the dog food proved a problem since his supply was at Nora's house and neither of us wanted to explore there without an armed backup. Eventually, after much whining, he sent me a recipe for dog meals that I could make from items in my pantry.

Half an hour later and much cooking, he had his meal and was ready to talk. "I work for Barkspace Security...contract basis...and before you ask, no I don't have an owner. I likely make more credits than you."

"That wouldn't be much," I said, my tongue voicing years of regret.

We were sitting in the living room. I on my chair by the fireplace, the one favoured by Nora, and Neep on the matching leather and dark wood footstool. The little dog looked about. "Yes, you have not done as well as expected, have you?"

"Thanks for reminding me. It was the Regen treatments."

"I have ReGen too. Easily affordable."

"Alright, enough showing off. What is our situation? Are we likely to be murdered in our beds?"

"Situation not good. Contract up in two days and I have another job."

"Hmm. Can you get out of it?"

"I will ask. Something else too."

"Yes?"

"Equipment damaged, and cost will be added to her bill."

"A lot?"

"Enough. We have no human scent detectors now."

"So?"

"So, that is how Neep caught bad man. Now can only smell him if he is close."

"I thought dogs could track people."

"Sensors and interface increase field of nose view. Interface broke when he banged my head on door."

"Oh…I see." I suddenly felt a twinge of empathy. He has a tough job. "What can I do to help?"

"Need to see a vet. Something not right. Need interface fixed."

"Alright."

"Can't walk far. Get me to vet. Here is her address. Call ahead."

The rest of the morning was spent in a waiting room as they did what they had to do. He came out bathed, coiffed, toenails trimmed, and with a bounce back in his short legs. I wished I had medical service as thorough. He must have noticed my curious look because he said, "Drugs." We were back home by lunch with a bag of luxury dogfood and some spare meds. He quickly set to work reassembling his security system. I was comforted. He was remarkably effective, but I think he needed a Doberman co-worker.

The women returned in time for my special lasagna made with durum wheat pasta and tomato sauce made from real tomatoes I had processed myself last fall.

"We brought back your bike," Darwina said as she removed her jacket.

"In one piece?"

"We rode it back. Good as new."

Neep scampered out the door, past Nora, barking as he went.

"What's with him?" Nora asked, a healthy flush on her pale face.

"The bike…the bike!" Neep yelled in our implants.

They left it in the sunroom leaning on the wall just inside the side door. That bike brought back memories. I patted its saddle as though it were sentient. "Welcome home old friend," I whispered.

But Neep had something else on his mind. He was on his hind legs, his nose smelling the saddle. "Bad man, here," he said repeatedly. "Look under!"

Darwina found it easily. It was electronic and stuck under the saddle. She removed it and stomped it hard on the concrete floor. "Oops, sorry I damaged your bike, Amir."

"Let's eat before the lasagna is cold," I said. "You can have some too, Neep."

***

We spent the afternoon fortifying my house. There was a storage shed in the garden packed with odds and sods. It was to be Darwina's next job when she had time between paying work. I knew there was wood in there, so the four of us got in each other's way as we hauled everything out making an instant disaster of Darwina's tidy garden. But we did find enough wood to protect the downstairs windows and doors. It was quickly done and looked it. Plywood screwed over the windows and boards set crossways on the doors like a medieval castle. But we knew this was not the answer, just a temporary fix to help us sleep at night. Neep reminded us with a list of methods of how they could defeat us, including beaming rays at us to drive us mad, smashing the doors with steel rams, and worst of all, setting the house on fire. I decided to block out his most horrendous scenarios. Fortunately, Neep's replacement parts arrived that afternoon and he was able to double the number of sensors, cameras, and electrified deterrents. By supper we were exhausted, but as ready as we could be, barring an all-out assault.

***

"When was the last time you cleaned and painted?" Darwina asked as she ran her finger over the wall's dusty surface.

"Feel free...but the paint must be special ordered. You can do the trim as well," I replied.

"When this is over..." she mumbled.

She had been inspecting my living room carefully as though for the first time while Nora snoozed in her chair by the fireplace.

"It would look nice in brown with black trim," she said.

"No. I like it as it is. Grey-blue with white trim is classic and goes perfectly with the dark-brown wood furniture and floors," I said, enjoying discussing this instead of security.

"I'll get some paint samples," she said as though she had not heard my response.

"Do that. And gold trim would be lovely too."

We had already prepared for our sex club meeting. That put Neep out of the loop, so he dozed by the fireplace on a pillow Nora had placed for him in consideration of his injuries.

"Been thinking," Nora said from under her sweater. "Where is this leading? What are our goals? Have they changed?"

"Simple, and nothing has changed but our understanding of it." Darwina sat close beside me on the leather sofa. Funny because she had previously insisted, she could not bear to sit on a dead animal's skin.

"Meaning?" Nora asked.

Darwina shrugged. "My friends say they have been manipulating our governance for some time. We came to experience it personally when Nora was accidentally placed on that citizen assembly."

"Agreed and she could've either cooperated or walked away...but didn't. Predictably, that's when things got bumpy...the library was burned down, Tattie implanted, and Nora's house broken into."

"And yet we have no proof we can take to the police," Nora added.

Darwina's hand flew up, almost clipping my ear. "And we've been playing defence for most of the game. I hate that! Look where it's got us? Holed up here like rats in a cage."

"We can always end this. We can let them know they've won, and we won't be further trouble," I said.

"Oh Amir, grow a spine!" Darwina said, glaring at me.

"Darwina, that was unkind. Amir has put up with a lot."

Darwina's insult had not bothered me, but Nora's comment had. My life had changed from living alone in harmony with myself to having my home filled with others. It felt uncomfortable, not that they were doing anything terribly awful, it is just that they were here, breathing, using space and my things, and even changing the smells. I was not used to it and it was unsettling. Had I become intolerant? Perhaps. It was then that I realized that this was like the time I was sharing a dorm at university. I hated it at first back then too, but it became the most exciting time of my life and when I met my wife. I was trapped in that maze of thought when Tattie and Rebecca arrived. They were late.

"Damned minibus," Tattie grumbled. "When traffic is

heavy, they make it worse by slowing down to walking speed."

"At least we were seated," Rebecca reminded him.

"Someone must've been touched. They always slow them down when there has been an incident," Darwina explained while sliding to the other end of the sofa. "Sit beside Amir, Rebecca. I think he's upset with me."

I was not but it was nice having Rebecca's warm body close. Darwina retrieved four crystal wine glasses she had discovered in the dining room sideboard. "They haven't been used for years, not since..." I started to say, then stopped myself reminiscing. "Go ahead, but you should rinse them first," I told her.

Tattie brought a few bottles of wine and placed them proudly on the coffee table. My newly cleaned glasses made that gay crystal tinkle as they were placed beside the wine. Tattie poured and served. Darwina fetched a platter of snacks then settled next to Rebecca on the sofa and took her hand. Tattie descended on the plush chair opposite. We toasted each other and sat smiling as though the serious business already had been settled. We could have let it stay like that till the wine carried us away to somnolent stupidity, but it was not to be. Darwina broke the calming spell. "Alright, Tattie. Tell us what happened at the church."

"It's not just the back implants, you know. They are doing something else, too...maybe pheromones in the air. I felt happy in there again, even with a broken implant."

"But you were caught," Darwina said.

"Yes, and I got out just in time too. They have a security system... a good one. Visitors get a tag that allows them in the public areas. The member tag gets you in more areas like the meeting rooms, the library, and so on. I received my member tag during the meeting with the elders."

"So, how exactly did you get caught, since I assume you were wearing your member tag?" Darwina asked.

"After the service, I noticed a group leave through a back door. It included some of the elders I'd met plus a few others, including a young man. I decided to follow them. It was easy. No one stopped me. They went into a meeting room and closed the door. By leaning on the door jamb, I could hear some of the conversation. It was about the library. One made a joke about it and the others laughed."

"That's proof of nothing. Many have laughed about it openly," I said.

Tattie smiled condescendingly. "There is more Amir. Then someone in the room suggested other targets of equal value to remove. I recognized his voice. He was the elder who questioned me. There were murmurs of consent, then the elder said, "But before we do that, Kevin, what are your plans to neutralize those meddling fools?""

"Kevin?" Nora blurted so loudly I spilled my wine.

"What is it Nora?" Darwina said.

"Oh God, not him! It can't be."

We waited for more. She set her wineglass down on the coffee table before she asked, "Tattie, can you describe the young man?"

Tattie shrugged, "He was the only young one...thin, wavy dark hair, perhaps part Asian. The others were much older."

Nora's mouth set. Her cold blue eyes narrowed. "If this is who I think it is, we are in a dung heap of trouble."

We were now fully alert. "Explain," Darwina demanded.

"Kevin Nguyen founded Xaltanium several years ago when he was a teen. For those who don't know, I work for Xaltanium. We are the ones who supply components for the interface software in our implant AI. But Kevin wanted to do more. He wanted to use the implants to influence buying decisions. He said it could make trillions."

"How so?" I asked.

"Well for example, a coffee shop owner could pay to have people walking nearby drawn into his shop, through suggestions and feelings introduced through the AI interface. I'm not sure how it worked but it was banned tech and the Board of Directors caught him working on it. He left under a cloud along with some of his team. That's how I got my job. I was a replacement for one of them. Anyway, I made a short-list of who had the skills to tamper with the citizen assembly AI and our thought messaging. Kevin was on that list but not at the top since I heard he'd left the area."

Darwina pushed on. "Then, let's assume it was him. Tattie were you able to identify anyone else besides the questioner?"

"Not directly. But I recognized some of them from my membership meeting. I looked up their names when I got back. The list is on this paper. There are five leading elders. At least we know now that the church elders are the ones behind the banned political activities."

"We might believe that, but we still have no proof," I cautioned.

Tattie set the paper on the coffee table. Rebecca picked it up and read the names aloud. I had heard of none of them before today. They were not prominent in any field.

"They are anonymous," Darwina mused.

"Precisely," Nora agreed. "But now we have names."

"The playing field has been leveled," Darwina grinned. "And before you caution us again, Amir. I know this isn't a game."

I nodded. "Damned right it isn't. And I still want to know how Tattie got caught and I ended up being chased into a freezing pond by two thugs."

"Aww poor Amir. Didn't like our little escapade?" Darwina teased.

I would've glared at her, but Tattie continued, "I was hanging near the meeting room when the security guy came by. He must have scanned my tag because he said there was something wrong with it and to please come to his office to have it tested. I was compliant, but at first opportunity I bolted to the side exit. I ran toward you, them in pursuit, then jumped on the bike and rode off. Then the GPS suggested a nice café nearby, just off the trail. So, I stopped for lunch."

"I'm glad you had a good time while Darwina and I were swimming for our lives."

Tattie smiled. "Well I can't go back, and I'll miss those happy feelings. We should get some of that pheromone mist or whatever it is for our sex club meetings. Might help Amir with his resentment issues."

Everyone had a good laugh at my expense. But I could not leave it like that. "So, let me summarize. The opposition includes an unethical AI software genius, and several members of the leadership of a popular church. They know who and where we are. For protection, we have flimsy boards over glass windows and a tiny dog who sleeps half the time."

"Good thing Neep didn't hear that," Nora chuckled.

"And by the way, we are losing even that bit of protection in a few days. Neep's contract is up, and he has another one waiting."

"I'll speak with him about it later. But I take your point, Amir," Nora replied.

Tattie's eyes blinked. "Our options are few but not negligible."

"My question is, do we have any options that don't guarantee we lose?" I asked.

Nora shook her head. "Not yet, Amir. Our adversaries are formidable, and they likely will expect us to come at them head on, like fools."

Darwina spoke next. "I think we should work underground. I mean literally and figuratively. Do nothing overt for now. Let's gather info about our opponents. Everything we can...without raising suspicion. I'll explore the tunnels under Guelph to see how we can use them. My friends will help with that. And there may already be maps in existence. Amir, can you ask around at the senior's centre?"

I nodded. "But we have to be incredibly careful doing all this. We don't want them noticing a pattern."

Nora agreed. "We'll be careful, won't we Darwina? Slow and steady. Mix it up. Take turns. I'll try to find out more about Kevin and his associates."

"And remember, we're in an extremely dangerous situation. Let caution be our watchword," I emphasized the last part.

"We can't just do nothing, Amir," Darwina blurted, the anger hot on her tongue.

"Sometimes doing nothing is the best strategy, Darwina. You may discover that someday when you've paid the blood price for rash behaviour."

Nora interrupted in time, "Alright you two. I agree with Amir. Let's not rush into this before we have a proper plan of attack. And before that we need a goal. What are our objectives? What do we want out of this?"

Rebecca squirmed beside me. I nodded for her to speak. "No one has done anything to me…so far. But my brother has been threatened and our government compromised. Isn't that enough? Our goals should be clear and simple, shouldn't they?"

"If there's anything worth fighting for, it's the little freedom we have remaining," Darwina exclaimed with anger.

"You exaggerate. We have considerable freedoms. It's just that you take them for granted." I reminded myself to refrain from lecturing, especially Darwina, so I left it at that.

But Darwina exploded with, "Yet they are encroaching and subverting. And I might add, they are breaking the damned law! Are we sheep or men?"

"Well, you most certainly aren't a sheep and likely not a man," Nora laughed then leaned forward. "I think we agree, we can't let then get away with this outrage. Rebecca is right, our goal should be clear: to stop them and bring them to justice. But we are weak, and they are strong. So, for now as Darwina suggested, lets cautiously gather information. Who knows what we will find? And we should also acknowledge that Amir has the most to lose and not just his home."

There was a pause. We seemed to be reaching a consensus, but I worried about where it would lead. There is good reason they say the road to hell is paved with good intentions. I hoped we were not laying the first bricks.

My anxious thoughts were broken by Nora, "How do you feel about it, Amir? We'll not force this on you."

"Feel? I feel like visiting my farm at Stardew Valley."

"You have a farm?" Tattie asked.

"Sort of…an imaginary one."

"We do too," he replied, "but ours is real."

| 8 |

Chapter Eight

"What the!" I exclaimed when he bumped my elbow. The offender bowed and apologized but instead of promptly leaving, he stood staring down at me a little smile on a curious face that resembled that of a crow with a long beak of a nose and beady dark brown eyes set in almost black skin. I was in my Iraqi coffee shop, but since the weather had turned raw, we were packed in the tiny interior so close that almost everyone was touching someone else. It was just as we preferred, like the old country of our fading memories. The man obviously had something further to say, so I queried, "Salaam brother. All is forgiven, may I help you?" in the polite way I had been taught by my dear mother.

The man bowed again and offered a digital calling card. I was immediately annoyed. First, he bumped my elbow, spilling my coffee, now he wanted to intrude in my mental space. But courteous citizen that I am, instead of telling him to go away, I smiled and read his damned card. It was a good thing I had not sipped some coffee at that moment because I would have spewed it on my neighbour since the card read: Special Agent Tony Rossi, Regional Ministry of Harmony.

My face must have registered surprise because he chuckled then flicked his head and said, "Come."

I had every right to refuse his order. But his peculiar appearance piqued my curiosity and I had nothing better to do, so I followed him out the door. We strolled slowly through St. George's Square. It was teaming with people going hither and thither, serious faces indicating the importance of their tasks. I think my face showed something different, a hint of fright perhaps, or at least a concern for my well-being as I tried to imagine the purpose of his mission. The special agent said nothing as he swooped through the crowd, wrapped in an overcoat made of shimmering black feathers that reminded me of Darwina's fly wing lips which she liked to wear.

The agent led me to a quiet area beside a car park turned children's fun area. I turned up the internal heaters in my clothing, regretting I had not brought a warm hat. He stopped and stuck a finger in his ear. I waited for him to say something. His focussed expression suggesting he was consulting his AI.

A quick bow and he began. "This is on the record. Everything we say will be recorded. You are not being charged with anything, but this is part of an investigation. If there are to be charges, they will be laid by officers of the Ministry of Justice and Reconciliation," Agent Rossi said from rote.

I blinked. At least my eyes were working if not my mouth. I stood there, mute.

The agent continued. "It seems you may have disturbed

the harmony field," his girlish giggle that followed not at all matching his scary crow face. He could have at least cawed for me.

"Ah...ahh," I finally managed to say, "Do I have rights?"

"They will tell you before you are charged. Were you not listening?" he replied.

I still did not understand, so I remained silent in the hope that the less said the better.

"Look, I will be frank. Your profile monitor has issued an alert and we must follow-up."

"An alert?"

He gave me a disdainful look. "Surely you know. Did you not read—"

"Of course, I know we are all being monitored. But why the alert? I have done nothing illegal...have I?"

"Behaviour does not have to be illegal to trigger an alert. The AI can predict when illegal behaviour *may* happen in future. We are here to guide you away from such before it is too late."

I had to take care of what I said next. We were being recorded. I had been duly warned. "Umm, OK. I am terribly sorry if my behaviour has seemed that way, but please believe me I have no intention of breaking the law...far from it. I am completely supportive of maintaining a law-abiding and peaceful society...that...erm." As I was speaking Agent Rossi's head began bobbing up and down. It was disconcerting because I was not sure he agreed with me or was about to mock my response. So, I decided to ask for clarification before I dug myself deeper. "Umm, agent, if you can tell me what behaviour of mine was going in an unacceptable direction, it would help me greatly to be a better citizen." His head stopped moving. He stuck his finger in his ear again and cocked his birdhead to one side.

His head jerked once and he said, "I am forbidden to give specifics but your over-use of exemptions and gaps in our surveillance system has been flagged, as well as your association with others who are known violators."

"Oh…oh," I mumbled. "If you mean—"

"I imply nothing. That is all I have been given. I leave it to you to change the course of your life before it is too late."

"I see. Well thank you Special Agent…ahh…Rossi. I will take that into account."

He bobbed his head at me again and said, "Then my task is done. I hope we have no further reason to meet." He lifted his arms and turned with a flourish as though to flap away.

"Wait!" I exclaimed. "I have a question."

He stopped in mid-takeoff, turned his head to me and nodded. I am not certain why I trusted him. Perhaps it was because of the rigorous selection process and training I knew they went through, and the constant monitoring of their emotional responses and psychological stability, or maybe it was that he looked so damned hideous that he had to be a good person. But for whatever reason, I felt I should take a chance. We desperately needed help and maybe he was it. "Can we speak off the record?" I asked quietly, hoping that would prevent them hearing.

He bobbed his head then said, "No. Everything is recorded. But we have finished our official conversation and we can have an un-official one if you wish. They have different legal standings; in case you are wondering. The official—"

"I get it and I would like an un-official conversation…if you have time."

He was agreeable and I told him in non-specific terms about our situation: that we may have uncovered a conspiracy, and that we are good people trying to do the right thing and may be in over our heads. While I spoke, he said nothing. I was becoming nervous and feeling I had made a mistake in confiding with him, although I had mentioned no names. So, I stopped talking and we stood staring at each other like an estranged couple. I was about to thank him politely and make a quick escape when he said, "I will be in touch. I need to consult others. Do I have your permission?"

My throat was dry. Do I trust him or not? I looked into his dark eyes and felt what? Compassion? Cunning? I sighed and nodded my agreement.

"I need you to say it…to protect me. Understand?"

I opened my mouth. All that came out was a croak.

"Good enough," he smiled for the first time then reached over with his arm-wing and gently tapped mine. He turned and surprised me by not flying off.

***

"Can they hear thoughts without our permission?" I asked Nora that evening. My paranoia level had risen exponentially since that meeting with Special Agent Rossi and I needed advice, but then worried that even asking about it would set off more alerts.

Nora was preparing supper in her mostly demolished kitchen. The sink emptied into a bucket that had to be emptied manually, but thankfully the water supply did work. She scrubbed some vegetables, rinsed them, then turned to me and spoke as though reading from a manual, "To access, one needs a wake word and on a deeper level, an encrypted password. I hope you change them often." She smiled, scrunching her face, and silently mouthed the word "careful".

Her answer made me even more nervous. Her implication being that everything is hackable, including one's private thoughts. Of course, I suspected as much, but it was one of those unspoken worries tucked away in that messy mental closet no one wishes to tidy.

I needed a sex club meeting badly, but that was part of the problem: too many meetings and so little sex that even the authorities noticed. And who the hell is the Ministry of Harmony, anyway?

"This will be a fine Irish stew. Rebecca is making bread for tonight too," Nora said in her best uninflected homemaker voice.

"I haven't had a good stew and fresh bread in a long while," I returned the pointless dialogue while scrawling a note with a lead pencil on paper that read, "We could be in big trouble!!"

The shape of concern formed on her mouth. "The protein is in the cold room, and there is a heavy box in the way. Can you help me lift it?" She canted her head in the direction of the stairs to the basement.

I replied with, "Of course, my dear Nora. Anything for you."

She glanced back and I could see by the glint in her eye that she was enjoying this silly play-acting. Her cold room is under the landing and entrance to her house. It is concrete all around but for the wooden door and about five feet square with shelving lining the walls. Nora clicked on the old-style LED light. Her shelves were mostly bare but for some potatoes, carrots, and onions in their respective sacks. There was no protein of course, but for our bodies that were so close I could feel her heat. "I think this might be safe in here," she said. "No signals I can detect, anyway."

"Just mine," I muttered.

She brought her head close to mine. "Tell me what happened," she whispered. "I sense you are upset."

I told her everything, including that I may have messed up by confiding in Agent Rossi. Nora gave a slight gasp when I mentioned that last part, or maybe she was having indigestion. When I had finished, we stood quietly. I wished we could stay here longer in this info-free cave and I imagined a fire on the floor and us cuddled around it for warmth.

"This may be a good thing," she said, ending my fantasy. "You should investigate the Ministry and make sure he is legit. That is your right. Meanwhile, I'll make discrete inquiries. As to your question about listening in on thoughts, I think it unlikely. They would have to filter out all the rubbish, which would be substantial."

"Thanks."

"I mean in general. But if they were out to get someone, it might be worthwhile. The government could do it with a warrant. But it's illegal for everyone else."

"Like erasing your family pics?"

"Indeed. But code words might slow them down."

"What do you mean?"

"Simple. Train yourself to substitute words in your mind. For example, Darwina is exploring the sewers. Instead of the word "sewers", she could say "shops". Wouldn't that be fun! I'm going to make up a substitution list today to share."

"Good. If it works and we are all using the same list."

"We will. And let's have a sex club meeting soon," she said, our breath mingling.

"Soon," I repeated. "I need it soon."

***

We did not have a meeting soon or at all, our unspoken fears and procrastination pressing us to make do with hasty whispers, coded words that most of us forgot, cryptic notes on scraps of paper, and when all else failed, brief one-on-one meetings in Nora's cold room. It all sucked and as the season slid toward the winter solstice, it became obvious we were becoming more apprehensive, not less, because of our efforts to maintain secrecy.

Some useful progress had been made though. Darwina often came home smelling like sewer. She usually was greeted at the door by Rebecca who seemed to have moved in with her. No one asked my permission, and I did not question it. It was fine with me because Rebecca was the best of us as a housewife and cook, pleasing us all daily.

Nora had fixed her broken window and door, and with her new roof was able to keep out the elements enough to continue living, or at least sleeping most nights in her reno house. The rest of the time she was with us, ensconced on my Poang chair beside the fireplace, often accompanied by Darwina and Rebecca on the leather sofa, with Darwina mocking the news displayed on the screen above the fireplace and Rebecca humming and knitting contentedly beside her.

Also, I knew Nora had been doing some research on Kevin Nguyen, based on the nonsensical notes she left everywhere for us to read. She seemed obsessed with him, perhaps rightly so. And speaking of obsessive, little Neep had become a regular visitor as well. He seemed concerned about our well-being, and according to Nora had refused any sort of recompense. I even offered him a home with us. His response was a loud snort sending dog snot on my pants.

As for me, if this was laying low then I certainly was doing it, and the most I had accomplished during this time was verifying the legitimacy of Special Agent Tony Rossi, although I still did not know how serious our situation was in relation to the government, nor had I any further contact with him. Some things are best ignored.

***

It was late and I had drunk too much wine when he rang the doorbell, sending Neep into a fit of barking. It was Imam Zia, the head of the Guelph Islamic Society. He was dressed appropriately in jeans, a t-shirt that read "God is Great!" and an electronic hoodie. His shaggy black hair was tied in a ponytail to complement a beard of twisted braids. He looked like a modern hippy.

He grinned, exposing rows of gleaming white teeth. "*As-Salam-u-Alaikum!*" he exclaimed using the traditional Muslim greeting.

I stood there like a dunce trying to think of the proper response. In the end I mumbled, "*Salam*", a question mark implied in my voice.

"Apologies, I know it is late, Amir, but I heard you have been having a spot of trouble and I'm here to help," he said using what remained of the British accent from his childhood.

The last thing we needed right now was a well-meaning, interfering Imam. But I invited him in and thanked him for coming to our rescue. It was the lesser of sins. He smiled and greeted everyone in turn, even Neep on his pillow with a paw shake. Darwina yawned and excused herself after asking Rebecca to serve our guest.

Rebecca was delighted when he accepted her offer of tea and cookies. I bade him sit on the sofa in the spot vacated by Darwina. Nora remained owlishly somnolent in her blanket by the fireplace.

Thankfully, the Imam got right to the point. "The leaders of the Church of Infinite Love have asked me to intercede."

"Have they?" I replied, my ears perking up.

"We believers work together for the common good. I know them quite well. They are decent people, Amir."

He waited for a response, but I offered none. I was not sure where he was coming from with this.

"I am not much interested in religion…not since…" I tried to explain.

"I know…since your wife's untimely passing."

Nora's eyes blinked open.

"Erm, yes."

"It has been a very long time, and we miss you," Imam Zia said in a voice sweetened with sincerity.

"Thank you…but what does this have to do with…that?"

He grinned and spread his hands, palms up. "Oh, I didn't mean to imply…it is just that we are all friends, and I am certain we can clarify any misunderstandings and—"

"Misunderstandings! This has nothing to do with misunderstanding, and if you are here in good faith to help, then you are being used…*sadiqi*."

His grin froze in place at my outburst. I suppose I was glaring at him too, but I had about enough of this whole situation.

"I…I can see you are angry."

"You'd better believe I am. We are held here like virtual prisoners, afraid even to speak with each other, and all because of that church and what they are doing."

Nora tried to caution me with a finger and eyebrows rising to the ceiling, but I had to continue. "And Imam Zia, if you are with them, if you are aiding them, you are *no* friend of mine."

"I was just trying…" he shook his head. "Amir, listen, when you are feeling more settled, call me. I believe I can help you and your friends." With that he rose and showed himself out as swiftly as he could manage.

A moment later Rebecca returned with the tea and cookies. Nora's face was flushed, and I must have looked as upset as I felt because Rebecca said, "He left? Well, have some tea. It calms the nerves."

I was about to explain my rude behaviour when Nora asked, "Your wife died?"

"Yes, long ago."

"I am so sorry, Amir. You told me how you met, but..."

"I know. I try to avoid the subject."

"Is it why you over-reacted just now with the Imam?"

"I suppose, partly...maybe."

Rebecca had poured my tea and offered it with cookies and a kindly smile. I took a sip and watched as she served Nora, thinking I should be more thankful of my friends.

Rebecca scuttled back to the kitchen. Nora leaned forward, steaming cup in hand, and said, "Do you wish to tell me about it?"

I almost declined but I suppose it had been unsaid far too long and Nora was so like my wife it made my heart ache when I looked at her. I started slowly, hoping her new-found empathy was real. I told her of my wife's dream. She wanted to be a nurse and help those in need. And her opportunity came soon after nursing school when we were newly married.

I stopped speaking when Rebecca returned. She looked at us both and asked, "Am I interrupting?"

"Amir is telling me about his wife," Nora replied.

"Ah, then I will be quiet as a mouse, or shall I leave?"

I thought it rude to send her away, so I smiled and welcomed her to be with us.

I continued the story, "It was the time of that dreadful virus. It had entered Africa to deadly effect. Doctors Without Borders put out a call for volunteers. She was beside herself with joy when they contacted her. I was heartbroken but supportive. Who would want a loved one put in harm's way like that? She left and three months later she was dead. Never got to see her again in person. Our last contact was a vid link. She looked awful. She's in a mass grave…"

Thinking of that time never failed to bring tears. This was becoming too emotional and I did not want to make an ass of myself, so I looked away and muttered a chant.

I heard Nora blow her nose and clear her throat. Rebecca sighed and whispered, "His wife looked like you, blond, fair. Darwina showed me a pic."

My head snapped back toward Rebecca. She was smiling warmly, her expression a loving hug. Nora sniffled and muttered, "Damned dust!"

"Time for bed," I said. "You may stay in the spare bedroom, Nora."

***

We had not seen Doctor Tattie in a long while. Rebecca assured us all was well with him and that he was swamped with work. I did not believe her. I had never seen his office busy, never mind swamped. More often it resembled a kindergarten during nap time. So, it was a pleasant surprise when he showed up for supper.

Rebecca had made roast chicken, with Nora having purchased a real frozen heritage chicken. It was a rare treat and muchly appreciated by us all. She served it with mini potatoes baked with olive oil and spices, and green beans slathered with butter. It made our tummies smile and put us in a happy mood.

"Had a *special* visitor at the clinic today," Tattie said without warning. "He was very *bossy*, but said he only wanted *harmony*."

I almost chocked.

"We need to have sex after supper," Nora said decisively. We all nodded in agreement.

"More chicken, Allan?" Rebecca said.

***

We were taking a risk, but this was important. Special Agent Tony Rossi now had contacted two of us. Tattie was rattled. There were subtle threats made and even more questions. "Did you check this guy out?" Darwina asked me.

"Yes, he's legit but his government pic made him look more…umm…human."

"He looked like a snuggly bear when he visited me today. I just assumed he was into cosplay. Then he flashed his ID and started asking questions," Tattie said.

"What did you tell him?" I asked.

"Only that I was a member of a legal sex club and that I'd attended that church. Not much more. When I was evasive, he laughed at me."

We were in the living room, all of us. Neep was playing with some new gadgets on the floor. We had dealt with our AIs and sound absorbers but that did not seem to be enough anymore, and we all seemed worried as Tattie explained what had happened.

"Did he give you the spiel about no charges being laid, and so on?" I asked.

Tattie nodded.

Darwina and Rebecca gripped hands fiercely as though anticipating a blow. Nora's head popped up and she said, "We mustn't be frightened. He's investigating, nothing more. And I have news too." She was about to explain when a thought message came. Neep growled. I swore. How is that possible with my AI communications shut off? But I recognized the voice. Was I going mad? I looked about the room. All eyes were on me, expecting an explanation for my curse. Then it happened again.

He said, "I know you are meeting in there. May I join you?"

I gasped then silently mouthed that Rossi was outside and wanting in. It was their turn to register shock. All but Neep who tore back to his control board and turned something on that instantly blew the electric power, leaving us screaming in the dark.

***

"I thought you said he was scary," Darwina whispered to me as Special Agent Rossi doffed his floppy yellow hat and fuzzy blue jacket.

"Yes...but he was an evil crow last time."

Rossi joined us in the living room, a silly grin stitched on his face and furry paws clapping approval. He looked like nothing more than a giant teddy bear.

"Changed your outfit?" I asked, offering him my seat. I joined Neep on the pillow beside the fireplace which was turned up high.

Rossi chuckled. "I dress to affect. Works well doesn't it?"

"I suppose a jolly teddy would not have frightened as much as a crow."

"Precisely!"

The others were observing our interaction intently, no doubt deciding if he was a threat. I was not sure either so I asked directly, "Why are you here Tony...may I call you that?"

"Special Agent Tony will suffice. I have news and wanted to meet and didn't want to frighten anyone…" he spread his arms as though requesting a bear hug. There were no takers, so he continued. "Let's start with the good news, shall we? First off, no one in this…err…shall we say for the purposes of accuracy, *political club*, will be charged with anything by the Ministry of Justice and Reconciliation…not yet anyway."

"Hey, wait! Our club has *nothing* to do with politics," Darwina said, almost shouting at him.

Rossi's teddy bear face widened in an imitation of a smile. "Oh, but it does…in the wider sense, and that is quite legal. *Partisan* politics are banned, not the private expression of political ideas and philosophies."

"So, we needn't have pretended to be having sex?" Nora asked.

"No. You could have just announced you were having political but non-partisan discussions." Rossi explained.

"Geesh," Tattie mumbled. "Then I predict attendance will slide."

"But it had nothing to do with having meetings, did it?" I asked Rossi.

He shook his over-sized furry head. "It was what came of the meetings, wasn't it? The monitors noted the meetings were suspicious because content didn't match title. Those get flagged all the time. In most cases it's nothing, just poorly selected titles, or descriptions. But in your case—"

"In our case, we did things that worried the field, or whatever you called it," Nora said.

Rossi nodded. "Our Ministry exists to maintain harmony,

and what you were doing was potentially a threat. We *had* to investigate. Understand?"

I for one did, but that did not make what we did wrong or improper. "And what about the reasons for our actions that we discussed a few days ago. Are there *no* valid reasons to disturb harmony?"

"Ah, I was coming to that. Normally one would report improper or illegal actions to the police, but on reviewing your case there was some acceptance of your actions among my peers, although the consensus was not in your favour. In the end, it was decided to warn and wait."

"We are thankful," I said. "And what about the overt crimes of others? What about them? They are subverting what little we have left of democracy, destroying our history, and much more."

A switch seemed to have been activated in his voice box because he went from teddy to grizzly in an instant. "Amir! Leave it to the professionals," he snarled. "This is being investigated, and we *do not* report to you."

I was expecting him to leap on me and bite my face. Darwina's hand slid down her pant-leg to her hidden knife. Rebecca was about to scream. Neep bristled at my side, but Nora had grabbed his multi-tool collar to restrain him. It was a stand-off. A bear against our political-sex club.

I held up my hands, palms toward him in appeasement. "Alright, alright. We will happily comply, won't we friends?" They all glared at me. "Ahh...umm. But I have a question if we are to go forward *harmoniously*."

Special Agent Tony made no reply, his eyes fixed on Neep

who seemed ready to launch an attack should Nora release him.

I continued, "To what extent are we being monitored. Are our communication streams being recorded? Can you or anyone else monitor our thoughts?"

Tony reluctantly pulled his eyes away from Neep. "As I may have told you before, intensive monitoring like that requires a warrant, and we don't have one...yet. You will be informed if we do. Every neighbourhood has a spin-tenna hovering above. You must have noticed them. They look like tethered balloons. They are used for your thought communications. And we use them as well for monitoring the harmony field. We know who comes and goes and if there are issues that need to be addressed. It was the spin-tenna that first alerted us to the discrepancies in your club. It also notified the police when Nora's home was invaded. I hope this information has allayed your irrational fears. We are here to protect and maintain community harmony."

While it was good to hear the government was not listening in, or so he maintained, I was becoming aggravated by his tone. "Yes, yes...peace and harmony, we get it. But what about the others? Can *other* people hack the system and gain access?"

Special Agent Tony's button eyes blinked. He thought a moment. "Ahh...all I am permitted to say is that the situation is fluid, and we are doing our best, and—"

Darwina exploded in a litany of profanities that stunned us to silence. Tony's bear head swivelled to her. I too swore under my breath then said calmly, "Thank you Darwina. I think you speak for us all. Special Agent, can you not see the situation in which you have us trapped? You have threatened prosecution and have provided nothing but words to defend us. There seems little separating you from our enemies at this point."

I think that outburst touched some neuron of compassion in his mind, because he said in a contrite tone, "I am so sorry…so sorry this has happened to you. Please believe me. But the main reason I came tonight was to tell you that there are actions permitted which are legal and acceptable."

Now I was the one taken aback. Was he here to help as we had hoped? I looked at the others. Nora nodded. Darwina sat back steaming. Rebecca and Tattie looked at each other and smiled. Even Neep's fur flattened. I took that as ultimate approval. "Then tell us what we can do that *is* legal and acceptable."

He was ready and listed the points one by one. But he could have given the same list to a troop of boy scouts. When he left, I felt deflated and by the looks on my friend's faces, they were having similar emotions. Even little Neep lay there with his nuzzle between his paws, sighing.

Darwina rose. "Welp, at least we no longer have to pretend we're having sex. Come to bed Becca."

Nora stretched. "Tattie, can you please sleep at my place. I'm still scared to be there alone."

"Sure thing, doll," he said winking at me.

That left me and the dog curled on the pillow by the fake fire. Life is like that sometimes. Could be worse.

***

"They are marked the same way as hiking trails," Darwina was pointing her finger light at the painted markings on the wall.

"Provided you can see them," I grumped.

"You should never come down here without a light, Amir. Told you that before, didn't I?"

"Hiking in sewers has never been a top priority."

"You need to pay attention this time in case you come alone. Look here. This trail has blue markings, and those three marks mean the trail starts here."

She had given me a map of the storm sewer system that criss-crossed Guelph, the sewers mostly following old stream beds, apparently. The trails were colour-coded, and the markings had different meanings. And she was right. I needed to know how to do this. We had entered an old sewer near where we lived. It was easy to get in, the iron door hinges having rotted off the concrete bunker-like entrance covered in vines that hid most of it. Darwina had explained that the sewer system had mostly been replaced by rainwater capture and the old sewers only used in extreme conditions. This sewer drained our neighbourhood and emptied into the Speed River behind the city water treatment plant. It was a good place to practise, she had told me, because few used it.

"It's not as spooky as the one by the church," I said as we slowly made our way.

"Much newer, and entirely made of cement pipe. We must watch out for dead critters and slimy messes of rotted plants, and such. They used to clean the sewers more often when they were in use. Here…look. These two marks mean there is a right turn."

There was barely room for me to stand upright. Darwina fit perfectly. The smell was not as bad as I had imagined. It was the feeling of being underground and closed in that un-eased as well as having my head constantly scrapping webs and crud off the ceiling. But petite Darwina was in her element, and I was glad she took the lead. "Not much further. I can see light."

"Thank the sewer gods," I said.

We approached the large metal grate. There was a pile of debris lodged on the inside.

"Not sure we can get out this way. I see a lock that looks intact." Darwina shook the grate. It refused to budge. "Guess that's one good reason few use this trail, and look up there, I see the marker that means this is trail end too. Very boring. No dead bodies. No treasure."

I pressed my face to the grate for a better look at the lock. "Hmm. But we might want to come back some dark night and inspect that lock from the outside. It looks awfully rusty to me. Maybe it will just fall off with some encouragement...in case we want to use this trail for something."

Darwina chuckled. "I guess you didn't take Special Agent Rossi's lecture seriously."

"On the contrary my little friend. I took careful notes. We can investigate, record, and report...and protect ourselves and our rights. That gives us tremendous latitude when you think on it."

"Yes, and I'm not giving up my dagger, and Neep stays till this over."

"Alright, and I'll keep my hockey stick. Now let's get out of here, I'm getting a chill."

"First, promise you'll explore the Woodlawn trail with me soon. I hear it is quite interesting."

I gave an exaggerated sigh. "Alright, but my pick for date night next time, OK?"

"You wish!" Darwina said. "Now maybe if Rebecca—"

I did not hear the rest because she screamed.

***

"It's settled then. We will speak openly?" Darwina asked Nora as we helped shovel broken drywall into a bin.

"You heard him. If we try to avoid surveillance, it increases suspicion. They don't like us doing that. For better or worse we live in a world where everyone and everything is being watched. We should've known they would catch us." Nora was looking extra cute with her face and hair dusted with drywall.

"We over-used our sex meetings, is all. They just want us to be open with them," I added.

"I don't trust them," Darwina said loudly. "And I don't care who hears!" She laughed and we followed with nervous snickers. It was funny, but not quite.

"Let's give it a try. We have our parameters and boundaries. We will know soon enough what side they are on." Nora stopped and leaned her chin on the shovel. "Did I tell you the police contacted me yesterday?"

I threw some pieces in the bin and straightened my back. It was hurting but I was too embarrassed to complain. There were some things ReGen did not fix and one was my back. Darwina and I halted and waited for more from Nora.

"They have the results of the blood and DNA tests from

the break-in. He is Hungarian. Wouldn't give me a name but he lives here in Guelph."

"And no arrests were made," Darwina added cynically.

"Correct. They have no direct proof he was the one who left his blood and DNA."

Darwina rolled her eyes. "I wonder how they managed that with all the surveillance?"

"Well at least they know who he is; and I'll bet he is under constant watch, as are we," I said.

"I should hope so. But just in case, Neep is installing extra nasty protection," Nora said forcefully, then gave the spintenna outside the finger.

Like an evil imp, Darwina grinned, "This could be fun…insulting our watchers all the time."

"Give it a rest, will you? Best if we go along to get along." They both looked at me as though I were speaking French. "An old saying," I explained using my best Gallic shrug.

Nora coughed and hocked up a white loogie. "I have more news, but it can wait. Let's get this done before I choke to death. This house is going to kill me."

We agreed since none of us had the proper safety gear and my health monitor would report me if I continued much longer.

***

"Amir and I are going to scout the sewer trails near the church, and…umm…other places of interest." Darwina had setup a view board on the wall of the living room and was lecturing us using a digital wand that looked like it was made for fairies. "Here and here," she pointed making the trails glow in their proper colours."

Rebecca held up her hand, "Can I come?"

Darwina blinked then smiled sweetly and said, "There may be many spiders, rats and slimy things. Are you sure, dear?"

"But you said the nearby trail wasn't so bad."

Darwina pointed her fairy wand again, showing pics of the inside of the trail we had visited. "It wasn't. But it's much newer and in use till recently. The storm sewers in the Centre Core and North End are *a lot* older."

Rebecca looked glum but relieved in that way she has of accepting life as it is. Nora is not at all like her. "Neep should go with you if he wishes. It could be dangerous, and we need a team effort on that one. And I hope he can install some gear near the church too, if you can get close without being seen." She looked down at him for a response, but he was either napping or studying digital wiring diagrams. It was hard to tell with him.

"Your attendance will be especially welcome Neep," I said.

Darwina puffed her mouth then agreed. It was all on Neep now. Once he was ready, we would go.

"Can I bring the tea and cakes now?" Rebecca asked.

"Not just yet, Rebecca," Nora said. "And by the way, where is your brother? We were expecting him tonight."

Rebecca's eyes widened. "Umm. I have been worrying—"

"She's been trying to contact him all day," Darwina answered for her. "He seems to be missing. We'll track him down first thing in the morning."

"Not like him—" I was about to say something about the church but Darwina beat me to it.

"If I find he's gone back to that damned church, I may kill him."

Rebecca's eyes widened further if that is possible.

"A figure of speech, Becca." Darwina chuckled and patted her hand.

But I was not so sure. Darwina seemed to be getting testier recently. We needed to act before she did on her own.

| 9 |

Chapter Nine

Next morning, I left Darwina and Rebecca to discover what had happened to Doctor Tattie while I went to mend fences with my local Muslim community and that meant Imam Zia. The Muslim Centre and Mosque is located in what was once a sprawling shopping complex on Stone Road which had been refitted with a minaret, a minbar and mihrab in the largest prayer room, plus areas for schools, meetings and the like. It was all redone in that glitzy Muslim boutique mall style popular in the Middle East a few generations ago and transplanted to good effect here. I arrived early to explore. The seasonal decorations had been placed, the greens, reds, and tinsels contrasting gaily with the gilded walls and Arabic scripts. It was an over-abundance of Islamic and inter-faith splendour, especially along the concourse full of shops selling every imaginable religious object from stone prayer beads to immersive virtual pilgrimages. It made me smile, my mind going back to that simpler time as a child when my life plan was yet in Allah's guiding hands.

Imam Zia's office was closest to the prayer hall at the

east end of the complex. I instinctively removed my outer-wear and took a seat among the others waiting. There were many but I had an appointment, precisely at nine o'clock. The walls were decorated with screens scrolling through short vids of important events and persons. I recognized many, including several featuring my father who was instrumental in purchasing this property during those years of chaos when real estate prices went almost to nothing. We had come to Canada with little and father's religious zeal had left us further impoverished. We survived, barely. I smiled at him and wished him well in heaven, or wherever good people go.

Imam Zia's AI greeter informed me that I was welcome to enter. The door opened and before me was his radiant face, arms outstretched, his body wrapped in a simple white tunic with embroidered trim. We exchanged cheek kisses then he took my hand and guided me to a patterned silk divan set behind a carved privacy screen. He touched a dot on the divan table. I noticed the air around us shimmer. We settled and he said, "Now we can speak privately. Would you like some coffee? It is Iraqi, freshly made for you."

I had come to apologize and hear him out, nothing more, and now this. "Coffee will be appreciated," I answered cautiously.

"I believe it is the brand preferred by your late father too, isn't it?"

I smiled, recognizing the aroma.

"He was a great martyr. We know what he did. It will never be forgotten," Imam Zia said with sympathetic certainty.

"I dislike martyrdom. It is often unnecessary." I smiled at

him. I knew my opinion on this made him uncomfortable. It went against the grain of tradition. I sipped my coffee and waited for him to come to the point.

"Umm...it is a manner of speaking. We wish our followers to live their faith as an example to others—"

"An example of sacrificing one's children for their religion?" I said, adding a cut.

"You seem bitter, Amir."

"Some traditions are beneficial, others harmful. But I am not here to debate theology. I wish to apologize for my inhospitable behaviour. And I *am* sincere. It was quite uncalled for, even under our—"

"No need, no need..." he waved away my apology. "We take our obligations seriously. Fostering harmony and goodwill between the religious communities is always our priority—"

"You had no choice. Religions would be banned, otherwise, like the political parties."

Imam Zia smiled warmly, "As you say. I am too young to remember those times."

"It's a hazard of living so long. One remembers too much."

The Imam paused. I could tell I was trying his patience. Not intentionally, of course. Well yes, intentionally. He had to be told the truth by someone.

"Let's back up a bit, shall we?"

I shrugged.

"When the ReGen treatments were first introduced, I understand it was quite a controversy. Some said it was immoral, others said that if it existed it was because God willed it." He stopped there, perhaps expecting an objection. I had none. "As I am sure you know, the Islamic scholars met and decided that ReGen was allowed provided that it was not done to avoid God's judgement nor heaven and hell."

"That had nothing to do with my decision, if that is your question."

"Ahh, good. It wasn't. But...but may I respectfully ask what was your motivation for taking the treatments? I see in our files, your wife died when you were young. Does it have to do with her?"

He had done his homework; I will give him that. He seemed a good man, on the surface at least, and trying to discover my motivations and if they impacted my present situation and whether he should help me. That is what I assumed, anyway. I decided to share, since he could find out easily enough with a bit more digging. "I worried about my wife's decision to work in Africa. The virus was spreading quickly. There was a vaccine, but the virus was mutating rapidly and there were reports that people who survived could be permanently damaged. Many women became infertile. You can read all about it in the histories if you want. Anyway, I reluctantly agreed that she could go provided she leave some of our fertilized eggs here in storage...just in case."

"I see. And the eggs?"

"They exist. I prayed and waited, hoping by some miracle she would come back, that the reports of her death had been a mistake." I looked away; the memories were hurtful. I sighed and turned back to him. "But in time I accepted it. Years passed and no other woman came into my life. Friends told me I compared everyone to her and that was unfair and unwise. Perhaps they were right. Then ReGen came along. I was in my forties. The techs said our eggs were viable. But I had no mate. And if I waited much longer, no one would want me, so I took a chance."

"Surely, there would have been someone?"

"Oh yes, a few of interest, but none who would carry my eggs nor tolerate what they called *my obsession*."

"Then?"

"The years passed," I mumbled, looking at the dark sludge at the bottom of my empty coffee cup.

His eyes glistened. He nodded once and said, "I will help you." Then he passed me a digital message.

***

"It was in the form of a read once file," I explained to them, "but I managed to memorize and copy it. I can send it to you."

We were having lunch. Rebecca had made a rather tasty fish-flavoured wrap. I had turned up the house heat when I arrived home, the wet snow falling outside chilling us. But now it seemed too hot.

"I'll have a copy too," Darwina said. Both women looked glum. I waited for the bad news about Tattie.

"Why did he give you this?" Darwina asked after reading it.

"He wanted to help. I think they are as worried as the authorities," I said in answer.

"We got the same list from Tattie. I guess that confirms it."

Rebecca opened the oven, and the fragrance of baked apples and cinnamon bathed our senses.

"Yes, it does. We know who and what, but not what to do about it," I said.

The front door alarm announced the arrival of Nora and Neep. We heard them shaking off snow, removing boots and piling outerwear in the closet. Even Neep had started wearing winter clothing, a quilted vest held on with magnetic snaps. The vest was rather fashionable, especially the patterns he could make appear with the touch of a paw. He seemed to prefer the digital camo ones. Typical.

"We have fish-like wraps and baked apples. Like some Nora?" Rebecca asked, her hand holding forth a large spoon as though to defend herself from the reply.

"Thank you, Rebecca, but no. Was offsite and ate already but Neep might like some leftovers."

That brought the predictable bark of approval.

Nora sat near me and got right into it. "Ok guys, what's happening? Got this file from Amir. Makes sense. How about Tattie? Did you find him?"

A look of pain came over Rebecca's normally placid face. Darwina muttered, "Damn him."

"OK, he's damned," Nora said and looked to me for elucidation. I shrugged, knowing little more than her.

"We are having a political discussion and don't want the nosey neighbours hearing," Nora shouted to the watchers. "So, go away. It is our right and we intend no harm."

Neep had installed more automation, so all it took was a thought and password from me and our security was turned on. He had even added sniffers to detect anyone trying to access us. Clever dog. I nodded, "It's on."

"I say we shoot that spin-tenna out of the sky," Darwina said.

"Let's do something less childish," I chided. Her response the predictable tongue pointed at my face.

I rolled my eyes ready with another mild rebuke when Nora said, "What about Tattie, Darwina?"

Rebecca served Darwina a second fish wrap then stood and waited for a response. "Welp, he's lying again. Found him at work. Pretended nothing was wrong and couldn't explain his absence. Didn't even respond to Becca."

"Doesn't mean he's lying," I said. "Maybe just doing other things."

Darwina grunted. "If he were in VR games or something he could have said so. But he was evasive, wasn't he Becca?"

We should not have looked at her because she was about to cry.

Nora spoke up, "I say we leave him for now. Maybe he doesn't want to be with us as much? Too much prodding right now might make it worse."

"Agreed. Let's leave this to Rebecca for now," I said.

Out the window, the snow was thickening, making it seem like a protective white lace veil had descended over us.

"Next," Nora watched as Neep attacked the plate of leftovers being offered by Rebecca. Nora chuckled then cleared her throat. "Our church targets have been confirmed by the Imam. Seems everyone wants them gone including most members of their church. And I have another piece of the puzzle. Kevin Nguyen."

***

I was up for some skulking. Nora said I was perfect for it provided Kevin did not have my biometrics in his security alerts. It was a chance we had to take. Nora could not do this. She was well known by him and any approach would have been flagged. So, it was up to me and Neep. I was using him for cover and his multitude of security systems on full scan. We looked a pair. Him in his new vest sporting a lively green hunting tartan design and a deer stalker hat with fake pipe. I was in my usual canvas winter coat, old fashioned galoshes, and a knitted toque. No one would have mistaken us for anything more than we were: an old man and his eccentric dog, harmless in every respect.

I was walking slowly using my pretend limp. We were at one of those commercial strip malls that had spawned when everyone liked to have places to gather in which to work. This one was largely abandoned; the old-style building materials gradually being sold for salvage. There were a few units near the minibus stop still in use. I consulted my notes again. It was number twenty-three. I tugged on the leash. Neep hated that, and I knew he would complain endlessly when we got home. But for now, he was the consummate professional, acting the part of a dog out for a walk with his master. Neep sniffed as I touched the entrance pad. It said in open voice: "Welcome to Nguyen Neurobiotics. Please state your business."

"Oh ahh, is this the place...umm...where my great-nephew Kevin works?"

There was silence for a moment. I said a prayer to the trickster god. The door clicked open. Neep and I staggered in. Neep told me through thought coms that all was well. No weapons detected.

No one was there. I looked about. The walls were bare and white, in need of a refresh. There were a few chairs by the single large window. I slowly sat, groaning and mumbling about my damned back. Neep decided to pee on the chair leg. I caught him in time with a scold. I thought I heard him laugh, little devil. We likely were being scanned, probed, and so on. I waited patiently in a pose of aged sleepiness. Eventually a human greeted us. She appeared slovenly in baggy clothing that hid a body unused to physical activity. I rose slowly to meet her, making a point of grimacing in pain as I straightened my back.

"You are looking for someone named Kevin?" she said, her tone sounding annoyed that she was the one having to do this.

"Yes, my great-nephew Kevin."

"You don't have a last name?"

"I do, yes," I said then nothing more.

"I mean Kevin's last name." She looked ready to clout me.

"Umm…he is…tall, last time I saw him anyway…but that was at the family picnic in…let me see."

The door to the back slid open. That was what I was waiting for. I let go of Neep's leash. I knew he would be recording everything as he sniffed and snooped while I distracted the man who had come out. It was Kevin Nguyen. I looked at him then back to the woman.

"I don't know you," Kevin said after he had a chance to sample my skin DNA as we shook hands.

"Kevin?" I said, acting confused.

"Wrong one, codger," he said, retrieving a hand wipe from his pocket.

"Shall I show him out, sir?"

I needed more time. "But, but can you help me? Kevin needs this." I too pulled a hand wipe from my pocket. But instead of using it, I held it before me as though it were an important message.

Kevin sighed. "Wait here. Glenna, can you quickly ask around to see if there is another Kevin working nearby. There are only four businesses open. Shouldn't take long."

She nodded. Kevin bade us goodbye and the sliding door opened again. Neep had slyly positioned himself to get a perfect view of the interior once the door opened. He was licking his nether parts as Kevin went by. *Not as smart as he thinks he is, but seems a nice chap,* I thought to myself as the door closed. I called Neep. The woman reported that there was no one named Kevin working anywhere nearby. She suggested I had the wrong address. We left as promptly as my roleplay allowed. One outside, Neep told me he had it all. And this time I swear he did laugh.

***

It has hard slogging, but everyone wanted a walk in the fresh snow, so we were bundled and booted, noses dripping, and calf deep as we forged a path like latter-day pioneers. Neep had joined us and was forced to hop like a bunny, his belly too low. It was Rebecca who seemed most in her element, rosy cheeked and wanting to sing old Christmas carols. She started. We did not join in. No one knew the words. She promised to teach us soon. Oddly, that made us happy. But everyone knew the real reason for our walk. It was to hear and discuss what Neep had found.

"I reviewed all his recordings," I said, warily scanning the woods. "They were definitely there...four Divine Life cradles. They had extra parts, too. Here are some pics."

"Neep said there were six humans present, by smell, although he only spotted four," Nora added.

"The other two likely were in the DL cradles," Darwina said. "And I've seen those versions before. The extra parts are food, drink and waste ports...for long-term use."

"I've heard you can get very skilled help if you offer perks like that, and many will pay for the privilege of working on a sexy project," Nora said.

"But why the industrial building? It would be much cheaper to rent a few pod homes at the university. They come fully-equipped," I asked.

"They must have proprietary tech they need to keep secure. Hence the building. There were rumours Kevin took intellectual property when he left Xaltanium. Nothing was done about it since the current owners wanted to avoid public scrutiny, or so I heard."

"But what's the connection with the DL cradles?" I asked.

"Ahh. Good question. And we need an answer."

"You said when Kevin was at Xaltanium he was working on something that would use our AI and thought implants to influence purchasing decisions," I said.

Nora smiled at me then said with a chuckle, "Your memory still works reasonably well. Yes, that is why he left. Strictly speaking that tech is illegal. The board thought so, anyway. Kevin disagreed, of course. I know they parted on frosty terms...threats of lawsuits and counter-suits, and so on."

"Then the church used similar tech to influence people like Tattie," I said, ignoring her taunt.

"Xaltanium doesn't have the implant tech they put in his back though. That's new," Nora said.

"Alright, we all get it. Let's trash Nguyen Neurobiotics and put an end to it!" Darwina blurted.

I wish I could have gagged her at that point. Instead I nervously looked behind hoping no one was close-by.

"Let's learn *Jingle Bells*!" Rebecca yelled loud enough to startle the squirrels.

"Tonight Becca, I promise," Darwina said, taking her hand.

"We must focus on what we are permitted to do," Nora said evenly.

"Find the link between Nguyen Neurobiotics and the church, and proof they are breaking the law," I said.

"Exactly," Nora said.

"And without us breaking the law," I added for Darwina's benefit.

Darwina laughed then said, "I think I know where to start...and don't give me that evil look Amir."

| 10 |

Chapter Ten

"We need to take it to them, make them uncomfort-able...then they'll make a mistake, and we'll have them," Dar-wina said with the certainty of youth.

We had entered a storm sewer on Woodlawn Road. It was the closest to the Church of Infinite Love and their com-pound. Neep was with us. He brought some ancient surveil-lance gear. "A mic and recorder," he said before we left.

Our goal was to get as close as possible using the sewers, then set up Neep's equipment and see what we get. Worth a try, we all agreed. But now that we were here, it did not seem so simple. We had come at night, and in the dark, it was frightening. And I cursed myself for not upgrading our finger lights. Even Neep seemed uncomfortable having to walk on the slanted sidewall to avoid the foul slop that had settled on the floor. This was much worse than our local tunnel, much worse.

Neep was in the lead, then Darwina who thankfully did not mind her role of clearing webs and God knows what else from our path. She was using her trusty garden hoe. "Anything can be a weapon," she said, quoting a survivalist manual. I had come equipped with an abundance of caution, plus waterproof boots, and a balaclava to protect my expensive ReGen face.

We had stopped so Darwina could consult her map. There was a confusing profusion of coloured trail marks on the wall. "Left goes north," she muttered. "Oh, what fun! According to my map that trail leads to a dead end. There used to be a cigarette factory beside a strip club there, with a tunnel running between. My friend told me that people would smuggle cigarettes from the factory to the club to be sold illegally. Want to explore?"

"No," I said immediately. Neep agreed with a growl. We had gone off AI thought comms, so the little dog was reduced to barks and growls. He had told me privately awhile back that he found it humiliating. Could not blame him after I tried it for a day.

"Your loss," Darwina said. "I'll have to come on my own some other time."

"No, you won't," I countered.

She made a rude noise with her mouth that resembled a fart. "Alright, boring old Amir. This way to the church...I think."

It was another kilometer or so, the church compound having been built on the site of an old golf course. "This should be it. Look, there's a manhole cover above us."

"And how do we know what we will face when we lift it?" I said, my nerves speaking.

"This part of the storm sewer serves the compound and the church. We should come up somewhere in the entrance road and what used to be a large parking lot," Darwina answered.

"We could have used Tattie's help with this. He's the only one of us who's been here," I grumped.

"Yep, but he's out of action and Becca doesn't know why."

"Let's wait a bit. See if we've been spotted. And remember if they come after us, we run like hell, OK?"

Darwina shrugged. I took that as agreement.

***

I was scrunched against the side wall when she poked me. "Time to go. Neep just said we were not under threat."

"Not yet," I grumbled.

Darwina whispered, "We need a few minutes out there so Neep can setup his gear. We'll be gone before they notice."

"Sure. Let's do this before I change my mind."

We had practised earlier in the day using our local sewer. Darwina and I would use the hoe to lift and move the manhole cover. Then I would lift her and Neep out of the tunnel. The rest was on Neep and the forces of good in the world, at least those who remained awake at this ungodly hour.

It took several heaves to move the manhole cover. All the while I was thinking something inside me might burst. But we did move the cover and I squatted so Darwina could climb on my shoulders. It worked at home in the light but here my balance was precarious in the dark and it took a few stumbles before I got her up. I glanced up and could see her looking around, the light from the buildings and outdoor lamps reflecting off her face.

"Hand him up," she whispered.

Neep was at my feet eager to go. I squatted again. My

knees cracked. He jumped into my waiting arms. This would be the worst, standing from a squat with a hundred-pound girl on my shoulders and a twenty-pound dog in my arms. My 128-year-old body refused to move. "Pull up when you can," I hissed up to her.

"Okay,' she said. I felt her body tilt as she raised her arms.

"Now!" I said. Neep seemed to levitate himself for a second. It was all I needed, that and a mighty heave that made my knees crunch. But we were up. I was feeling light-headed but competent enough to lift Neep up to her. She let him loose. I could hear his claws furiously tear into the pavement. She pulled her weight off me using the rim of the manhole. I took some deep breaths to recover.

It suddenly became very bright. Darwina cursed and called Neep back with a whispered shout.

"Down!" she yelled at me.

I tried but it was rushed, and I lost balance. We ended up in the sludge on the floor. I was disoriented. Darwina scrambled to her feet. "We tripped the security lights!" she said, searching for her hoe that she had left propped against the wall. My muscles were trembling, my elbow smarting from hitting the floor, and I was covered in stink. But for some irrational reason I was elated. We had done it!

Good sense soon enough took over and I yelled, "We need to get out of here. Forget the damned manhole cover!"

Darwina lead us with her finger light, running, hoe in hand. Moments later I heard someone behind us, the sound of footsteps louder with each step. "Faster," I gasped. I looked back. There was light behind us in the tunnel and Neep was failing to keep up, his vest and equipment catching on debris. "Darwina!"

She slithered to a stop and swiveled to face me.

"Give me the hoe and take Neep. I'll stay and hold them off."

"No! We face them together." Neep yapped his excited agreement.

We had no time for argument. "At least give me the hoe! You have your dagger."

We crouched low, each taking a sidewall. It was one person coming toward us fast. Neep growled. "Not yet boy. Wait for us to move first."

The light was blinding when our chaser turned into our tunnel. He must have seen one of us because he stopped dead ten meters or so away. He searched with his light, then stopped on Darwina's face. "Come out of there. You were trespassing. Turn yourself in," a waver of fear and adrenalin affecting the female voice.

Darwina stood to face her, "We were *not* trespassing. That was a public street, and we were under it. It is not church property," she said defiantly then took a few steps forward.

I held my breath, hoping the woman would leave. Instead, she mumbled something then there was quiet. *She is asking for backup in her comms*, I thought. *She'll stall till they arrive.*

I launched myself and gave her a whack with the hoe on the way by. She yelped and went to one knee. Neep did his best wolf imitation close to her face. Darwina revealed her dagger.

"Run away!" I growled at her in my most fearsome voice,

poking the hoe at her like a spear. "Get out of here!" I did not have to suggest it again. She scuttled back. But she did not go far. She must have known what I suspected: that there was someone else coming from the other direction to help her. Darwina had her lights trained on the woman. I whispered to her, "They think they have us trapped. We should go back to where we entered and *over* whoever is in our way. Got it?"

Darwina grunted.

"You lead. I'll have our backs with Neep. Go!"

And of course, I was right. But not quite. Instead of one man confronting us on the way back, there were two: the men who had chased us on our bicycle adventure. And they appeared much larger within the confines of the sewer. We had been running slowly. Darwina glanced back at me when she spotted them. I sprinted past her; my hoe out front like a lance. The men stopped and crouched, one on either side of the sewer. The larger one laughed. The other said something rude. I believed they would try to bat my hoe out of the way then jump me. As I ran toward them, I imagined my moves and repeated them in my mind, one sequence per second. Beside me Neep was galloping at full charge, his barking sounding more like a primeval screaming wail. At the last moment, I turned my hoe sideways at hip level. We hit them at the same time. My hoe catching them both in the upper body as they rose to grab me. It sent them falling backwards and me head over heels, the breath punched out of me, the pain searing my abdomen. Darwina leapt on one, her dagger to his throat. Neep sunk his teeth in the other man's ankle, shaking it like a rat, trying to detach it from his leg. *He must be the one who hurt Neep in Nora's house,* I thought, shaking away the stars in my eyes. Neep's victim was screaming in pain and trying to punch Neep. I got to my knees and hit him hard with the hoe handle. We readily subdued them with hoe, teeth, and dagger. Unarmed, they had little choice but to surrender or risk further abuse.

The woman following us arrived seconds later. "Stay away," I told her. "It's over. Your men are unharmed. We won't press charges if you won't."

She must have relayed that because a moment later she said, "Let our men go, and you can leave."

Darwina turned her finger light to both men's faces, recording their images. We watched them hobble away, no doubt humiliated and hurting. After they had gone, Darwina whispered, "Now that was satisfying."

I thought so too.

Neep's little tail thrashed the air as he barked our opponents away.

***

"It uses encrypted analogue burst transmissions when we activate it; very old tech from the last century," I explained to Nora as we walked down Woodlawn Road with the receiver/recorder in my pocket.

"My hands are freezing," Nora replied.

We were carrying stuffed shopping bags, as though we were returning from an outing. "Here, have one of my mitts." I offered it to her. Her head shook and she said something about it being her fault and why should I suffer.

We were headed up the hill past the church compound

and toward the residential complex beyond. It was time to turn on the receiver/recorder. We stopped walking on the bridge crossing the river. I pretended to shift my shopping bags and fumble in my pocket for a tissue. Nora was standing still, her body towards me but watching the entrance to the church compound ahead. I pulled it out of my pocket and pressed the button. A light glowed blue.

"It's done," I said.

"No one around," Nora whispered.

"Let's head back."

"I know a warm place nearby which serves hot chocolate, and I think there is a minibus stop out front," she turned to go, not waiting for my agreement.

"I'll buy," I answered, trotting to catch-up.

***

It was one of those franchised shops that had proliferated like lawn weeds. It sold every form of legal drug available: caffeine, alcohol, THC, CBD, DMT, and many others whose scientific names had been reduced to friendly marketing acronyms. The booths were synthetic bubbles with an order panel on one wall with a slot from which the products were served. Nora fiddled with the atmospheric panel and we found ourselves surrounded by a rain forest and a band of annoying monkey sounds. I asked her to turn off the monkeys and leave the soothing water drips. She turned up the monkeys, then laughed.

Monkeys thankfully stifled, I shrugged off my winter coat and ordered a large Brazilian coffee, double soy milk. We faced each other across a table image of primitive wood planks, the poor resolution too many generations old. But it was nice to be warm and alone. She ordered her cocoa, the ancient version with hot peppers, no milk. She smiled and said, "I have exciting news."

"More exciting than spying?" I replied in jest.

"Much more...Amir, I think I met someone!"

She proceeded to tell me about him. I listened patiently, even asking a few questions to show I cared. Why do women do that to men? In any case, he sounded perfect for her. Intelligent, handsome, tall, good job. He could have been her brother they seemed so alike. It saddened me and I knew why. It was as though my wife had told me she had found someone new. I know, it is completely irrational, but there you have it.

Then she abruptly changed topics. "But what I wanted to discuss was ReGen. He's on it you know."

"Uh huh," I said.

"I know all about the tech. It was easy to research. But why do people do it? I know the obvious reason...to live longer...but beyond that...why?"

She stared at me with an earnest expression suggesting she really did want an answer. I collected my thoughts. "You are asking about motivations, and those vary considerably, person to person."

"And what was yours?"

It was the question I had been dreading. The answer lay deep in my soul, hidden, unrevealed, even to myself, through most of it. "I...I..."

"Has it to do with your wife?" she asked carefully.

"It's not easy to discuss and it may seem foolish. But no, it isn't entirely about my wife, although what happened to her initiated it."

She squinted her eyes at me, her expression making her look older and wiser than her years. "I need to know. It's a big decision."

I assumed she meant she wanted to know about me. Few can resist an expressed interest in their lives, so I told her about my feelings of incompleteness. Most everything of importance to me has not been finished. "Imagine you are an artist and worked your whole life and never managed to create what you could see in your mind's eye. Imagine you are a writer and failed to write a really good book. It's like that."

"But you aren't an artist nor writer."

"Still."

"So, you failed to complete some things. We all do."

"I know it's all a matter of perception. One person's failure is another's success, and so on."

I waited for her to delve more deeply into the reasons for my feelings. What specific things had not been completed, and so on. And the deeper issues of incomplete love, family, and loss. But she did not ask.

"But what does this have to do with ReGen?" she wondered aloud instead.

I shrugged. "Simple, I wanted more time and hoped in time that failures would become successes."

"But they didn't."

"No. Not yet anyway."

She laughed. "So, you are saying that hope is what keeps you on ReGen."

"I suppose to some extent. I think now it is mostly habit. It's hard to imagine myself aging. It frightens me, to be honest."

"But what if ReGen keeps us from something better? Isn't that what many religions believe?"

"So, they say, but the existence of an afterlife has never been proven."

"Nor disproven."

"One cannot prove non-existence."

She sighed. "Philosophy 101. I hated that class."

"That's why I chose ReGen. At least it was real, and I could afford it."

"Amir, I am starting to see myself changing…aging. And now I may have found a mate and a reason to care."

"I understand fully. It's a big decision. And there often is a downside too."

"Such as?"

"Such as opportunity cost. You may have to give something up. And then there is the community. Many are jealous or disapprove and call us names."

"Like codgers and riders?"

"And worse. The harassment and prejudice. You may have regrets and wonder if its worth it. Discuss this with Tattie. He's the expert."

She reached across the table and took my hand. "Thank you, Amir. You're a good friend."

I nodded. I was good at friendship if nothing else. The warning flashed that our allotted time in the booth was almost up.

***

"I'm going to need some help with Kevin. Amir's probe into Nguyen Neurobiotics checked out. They are doing something in Divine Life, but I don't want to risk my job nor company going after him there," Nora said to Darwina when we got home.

"I have friends who play there. We did that job for Amir." Darwina looked at me and smirked.

"A successful one too, I might add."

"But that was much easier than what you want. For it to work, we would have to be selected to participate in whatever they are doing. Not the same as a simple trolling campaign."

"Can we at least try? Maybe we'll get lucky?" Nora asked.

"And while your brattish friends are snooping in DL, have them do a search of church groups operating locally," I suggested.

Darwina agreed. "I'll ask around. See if anyone is interested. Some credits would help too, and I'm broke."

"Just sent you some. Is that enough?" Nora asked her.

"More than. Can I spend the rest?" Darwina watched for the reaction from Nora, but there was none.

"Geesh, she's mellowed," Darwina whispered to me.

"Yes, and for good reason," I replied.

Darwina raised her eyebrow, no doubt wanting more but I walked away. I had received a message from Doctor Tattie. He wanted to see me today. It was urgent. I may have missed my December treatment. I doubted that were true, but I flung my coat on and headed out into the cold.

***

Tattie was good at doctoring, so it was strange to see him behaving as though he had never seen a syringe before today. I had tried to engage him in polite conversation, to no avail. It was all business, and poorly performed. "I...I had better give you this...whatever it is," he said, sweat droplets forming on his temples.

I was thinking the obvious, that he had been implanted again and being controlled by the church. And did I really want what was in that syringe injected into my body? Not bloody likely. "Ow, that hurt!" I said, even before he started. He nodded with an almost imperceptible smile, squirted the syringe into the wastebasket and placed it back on the tray.

"That'll do till January. I apologize for the mix-up of appointments. You should've had this one last time," he said while searching his pants pocket.

"No worries," I said, watching him retrieve the small paper envelop.

He handed it to me and said, "Here, eat this if the treatment upsets your stomach."

"Umm, Ok," I mumbled, searching his face.

He tilted his head in the direction of the door. We said our curt goodbyes and it was over.

Outside, on the street, I opened the envelope. Inside was a sheet of paper, folded many times and filled on both sides with penciled writing. The first line said, "I may be able to obtain proof that the church burned the library, can't meet; they are watching."

***

"Tattie seemed scared," I told them that evening.

We had decided to meet in our local sewer, the only place secure enough to satisfy Darwina's growing paranoia. It was underground, big enough for us all, and Neep had installed sensors throughout. "We own it now," Darwina had said when Neep finished. She was right of course, none of us honestly believed our home security had not been compromised by our helpful government, or even worse, by our opponents. The sewer would have to do for now.

"It was the weird shadows that caught me off-guard before," Darwina explained as she led us to a dry spot where we could sit. "That's why I screamed. You would've too. Looked like something out of a horror vid."

"I hate this," I heard Nora say to Neep who seemed happy to be having another outing.

"This is it Becca, no sludge, no bugs," Darwina said tossing the cushions down.

Nora decided to remain standing "Let's get this over with. Been a long day."

I trained my light on Tattie's letter and was about to read but Nora interrupted, "The short version, please."

"Alright. I can let everyone read it in full later. Tattie has a close friend he does not identify." I looked over at Rebecca. Her face was blank, so I continued, "His friend joined the church and allowed him or herself to be implanted. Tattie removed the implant and disabled the interface connected to his friend's nervous system. He also added a chip to record signals sent and received. Tattie said these are the signals used to control people and he has them…he has recorded proof now."

"He always loved playing in the lab…" Rebecca said.

"But what about the library?"

"He said his friend is willing to go back in and get some proof the church was behind it."

Darwina shook her head, "That'll be dangerous, especially after our recent encounter in the sewer with their guards."

"Agreed," I said. "Tattie and his friend have taken enough risks. What they managed to get is good evidence to add to our case. I think they should grey-out for a while and leave it to us."

We all agreed.

Nora was looking around, an uncomfortable grimace on her face. She asked, "Anything more in that letter?"

"Lots of technical details about the implant. The one we retrieved from Tattie's back was destroyed, so it will be useful to have an intact version to pass along."

"To whom?" Darwina asked.

"I assume once we have enough good evidence, we'll give it to Agent Rossi or whomever he recommends."

Darwina puffed her cheeks in disapproval.

"I hear you Darwina. It won't happen without everyone's approval, OK?"

"We aren't even close to having a proper case against them yet. So not worth discussing," Nora said, brushing imaginary bugs off her pants.

"Tattie ends his letter with a request that we protect Rebecca and asks for our understanding and...kindness...and that he thinks it best if he stays away."

There was silence but for the sound of water dripping in the distance and wind through the sewer grates. It was creepy yet soothing. I was beginning to understand Darwina's attraction to it. Nora obviously did not concur and was the first to leave.

***

We decided that Rebecca should be the one to convey our love and warnings to her brother. But also, we decided that we had to press on with our inquiries. We would be working on three fronts: using Darwina's friends to infiltrate Nguyen Neurobiotics in DL; monitoring church activities with Neep's surveillance gear; and using my contacts to shake the trees and see what might fall out. To that end, I decided a visit that evening with the Imam was in order. All he had given us so far was a list of names that merely confirmed what we knew. Surely, he had more than that.

The Imam lived on Steffler Drive, in one of those reconstructed neighbourhoods built after the student riots. It was convenient to the Mosque and was a salubrious place to raise a family.

"Greeting, sir. May I help you?" his security system said as soon a I crossed the property line.

"You may access my ID," I said in return.

A moment later the front door opened, and an elderly woman dressed traditionally in a chocolate brown hijab bowed and bid me enter. She looked at me questioningly. I smiled and said, "*As-salamu alaykum.*" She looked familiar in that way many older women do.

He was playing a VR game using a pair of lenses linked to his AI implant, and removed them as soon as I entered. "The latest soccer sim is amazing," he said pointing his head to a spot on the sofa for me.

"I know...especially the ones where you can play in the style of famous footballers through the ages. The contrasts can be hilarious."

"You play VR soccer?"

"Used to…then the leagues became over-run by idiots, and I left."

"Oh, they cleaned that up. It's safe to come back."

We chatted amiably about virtual soccer for a few minutes, but we both knew I was not there for male bonding.

"We thank you for the note," I started. "It confirmed what we already knew."

The Imam shifted to face me. "I am glad it helped," he said cautiously.

"Are we OK, here?" I asked.

"Yes, but for my family. So please be moderate and kind in your speech."

I smiled. "What I don't know is what you expected me to do with this info."

He thought a moment, the wan smile never parting ways with his face. "I and our community want harmony and peace to prevail."

"As do we all. Now how about specifics?"

He reached back and touched something on a small control panel in the sofa. "Extra precautions," he muttered.

I continued, "I believe we are on the same soccer team. We just need to find a way to work as one. We need less solo and more multiplayer gaming. Don't you agree?"

His smile broadened to a grin and he said, "Yes!"

With that, he started carefully explaining the dynamics of interfaith interactions. They were complex and subtle. Everyone has freedom. Everyone is being observed to ensure it. Each year there are several scheduled interfaith events. All faiths must participate or risk the censure of our government overseers. Within that framework all could thrive in safety.

At least that was the hope. But occasionally there were ripples in this field of religious harmony. And it seems now we have a ripple that must be dissipated with the calming balm of wisdom and forbearance.

"I understand fully. And you don't want this ripple replaced by another, namely us."

"You could say it that way, but we prefer to see you as less than a ripple."

I laughed. "Well, the Buddhists imagine us as no more than bubbles in the sea, so I get your point."

"I apologize, it was not my intent to diminish your existence. All are important in God's eyes."

"Back to the question at hand. You think we have a ripple. I say it could be a rogue wave that may drown us if left unchecked. They are subverting the very government that keeps us safe and our religions able to exist." I waited for some form of agreement. He reformed his wan smile and said nothing, so I pressed on. "Imam Zia, with all respect, the authorities including you have been less than helpful, providing not much more than platitudes. We need real and effective assistance. Are you willing to help us? If not, I bid you good day."

I think he did not appreciate my aggressive approach. His mouth twisted as if sucking a sour cherry. He touched that sofa panel again, cleared his throat and said, "Alright. Yes."

***

"A good thing about being so old is that I can always claim *cogno dementia* or terminal grumpiness as an excuse for improper behaviour," I said to Darwina and Rebecca when I returned.

"In your case, it would be true," Darwina teased.

"And now we know what to look for to close the case," I added. "We just have to get in there and get it."

I had told them about my conversation with Imam Zia and what he knew about the burning of the library, that he believed it was to cover up a massive theft of records that included the library archives, and that he thought the church group intended to use some of these records to blackmail and control people. "Proof is power," he had said misquoting someone.

"The only way in is in," Darwina said, "and how do we do that without breaking the law?"

"Maybe that's why they need us. We are expendable and easily disavowed."

"Geesh, you are becoming as cynical as me," Darwina giggled.

"One of life's lessons. The innocent lambs get slaughtered."

Rebecca blinked then said that she had passed on our love to her brother. We both knew that mean she had included our wish that he should back-off.

"It's late. We can discuss this more in the morning," I yawned.

"Oh, I forgot to mention that my friends started our little project in DL today."

"Yes?"

"As it happens, no infiltrating was required. Kevin's group, under another name, were doing marketing research for a new product and anyone could take the survey. And guess what it was for?"

"Hmm…something that involved an implant in your back?"

"They didn't mention implants. Their survey asked questions about how much you would be willing to pay for a product in real life that would make you feel happy, or loved, or pain-free, or even sexually satisfied on command. And…and…get this. It could be used in combination with Divine Life too."

I thought a moment. It was an obvious product extension. "They would have users addicted in no time, and completely at their mercy," I said, thinking out loud.

"I suspect so. The major deficiency in DL is that there often is a disconnect between the visual/audio experience and what your body is experiencing. That's one reason many people end up leaving. It's disconcerting to be having an experience that should be joyful when your body is in pain…and few want to risk taking drugs."

"Any sense of how their project is being received?"

"Apparently quite well, as long as it's safe."

"Hmm…they've had many test subjects at the church, haven't they?"

"Yes, and here's the kicker. They intend to market this as a better way to live than using ReGen. Why have an overly-long, tedious life when you can have a perfect one? And it will be much cheaper than ReGen too."

"Or better yet, a long, perfect one."

"For the wealthy few, I suppose."

"This is going to rattle more than a few cages. If it works, it could change everything."

"And make Kevin Nguyen the richest person on the planet."

"Indeed, and his backers," I said, my mind reeling.

I suddenly felt very tired and every year my age. I needed a nap. I needed to forget. I leaned back in the Poang chair by the fireplace imagining I was Nora in her bulky wool sweater. My eyes closed.

"And guess who else my team ran into in DL?" Darwina said, halting my calming reverie.

I opened my eyes. Darwina was smirking at me. I expected the worst. "Well go on, tell me. I can use more bad news."

"Your blood sucking friend, the Asian cross-dresser."

I only knew one person who fit that description. "Zhang Lei?"

"The same, new and improved too. And looking to hook up with another of your sleazy friends."

"Oh, for heaven's sake!"

| 11 |

Chapter Eleven

I never quite bought the allegation by Lei that Ranjit had ripped him off too. They had been long-time DL lovers and both in need of credits to fund their desires. Made more sense that they would work together for common benefit. I have since discovered on reporting it to the authorities that I was the only victim of that scam. And I have heard nothing much about either of them till now. So, if Lei has surfaced, a check on the whereabouts of Ranjit was in order.

I strolled into the senior's centre next day, stood in line for ages at the antique security booth while each and everyone entering had to tell their life's story to the bored guards, then I asked at the front desk if Ranjit had been around lately. The woman had that expression of having seen every scam imaginable in her short life and did not care. "You're that friend of his, aren't you?" She squinted waiting for my answer.

"Friend? Ah well we were, then he left. Heard he may have returned and want to see him," I said being perfectly truthful.

The woman scowled, "Alright, he's had a lot of people asking and we don't give out personal info. Why don't you try messaging him instead of taking up my time?"

I forced a smile, "Quite right, apologies. I won't bother you further."

She scowled and looked down to her screen.

"Oh, one more thing. I would like to clear any of his debts here if there are any."

She glanced up abruptly as though surprised I was still there. "Oh? Why?"

"As a courtesy. He did me some favours, and—"

The woman slid her finger over the screen, then said, "No need, he's paid up and placed a significant deposit a few days ago."

"Ah, good, well I'll be on my way then. Thank you for your help."

I needed to think, and it was too cold for a stroll in the nearby park, so I jumped on the waiting minibus going downtown. There I wandered through the indoor mall filled with boutiques where one could rez virtual samples to inspect before purchase. Most products from these shops were printed on demand locally and delivered same day. All but expensive craft items like the hand-knit wool sweaters Nora wears.

Shopping is a mindless way to spend a morning and let one's mind organize possibilities. It had only been a few months since Ranjit had bolted with my credits. I thought I would never see him again. What was he up to? I had to find out. But knew that one could easily be re-victimized by the same person. He surely knew that too and perhaps would dangle the possibility of getting my credits back as bait to finish emptying my savings. I had to be careful. I also had to control my anger. But there was the opportunity of restitution, or revenge, or the satisfaction of closure, and maybe something else.

***

Next morning over coffee, Darwina went over it again with Nora. Eyes drooping, Nora merely murmured, "So that's what he was working on. No wonder he left under a cloud. That could be an amazing product if it were legal."

I had all night to think on it, the pros and cons. "Maybe it could be legal...parts of it anyway, but under supervision. Could be a wonder for some people."

Darwina disagreed, "But not in his hands. I don't trust anyone with that much power."

"That's the issue, not so much the tech," I said.

"Speaking of people with too much power, Neep's sensors have been picking up some interesting chatter," Nora said after a generous gulp of coffee. Neep was busy playing with a plush toy which unfortunately had a squeaker, so it was up to Nora to explain further, reverting to her bizarre code, of course. I kept my notepad close in case I needed to translate.

"Last night's *starlight* provided insight into where our *constellation* might reside," she said slowly pronouncing the words.

"I am so sick of this," I grumbled, looking up the nonsensical words.

"What?" Nora said, turning to me.

"Next time we meet in the sewer," I answered.

"I hate it there," she said.

"And I hate doing this."

"Here, I'll write it for you, lazy boy."

"Fine, do that," I grumped. Rebecca thought I needed more coffee. She was probably right.

Nora's note came back as "Last night's recordings provided insight into where our target might reside." I sighed and said, "No one listening would understand that either."

The breakfast meeting went on like that for a while, each of us testy and uncooperative in our own way.

***

Surprisingly, Neep's sensors had not been detected by the vigilant folks at the church and continued to provide snippets of info that indicated the library archives might be stored in a locked room under the church meeting hall. They were behind a locked door, recently labeled "Hazardous Materials" and the subject of ongoing verbal curiosity among the staff. That combined with Tattie's evidence of exactly how churchgoers were controlled with those back implants, and we were beginning to build a convincing case for premeditated wrongdoing. It was time to visit Agent Rossi before we took the next steps.

He directly invited me to his home, located in what was once a large insurance building downtown, insurance having been abolished along with countless unnecessary businesses during the difficult times. The building was a maze of garish corridors, seemingly decorated by someone who specialized in designing fun parks. But these were not new and virtual like Ranjit's apartment, rather it was old and dingy with faded paint and flickering lights. I laughed and thought it the perfect place for Agent Rossi and his penchant for weird cosplay.

There was but one door, painted purple and black with celestial signs and a large moon which seemed to be a one-way view port. He opened the door before I asked his AI. He was outfitted as a spider with dots for eyes and too many useless floppy legs. "You look daft," I said on entering.

"Working on a project," he said.

"To trap someone?"

"Something like that."

The apartment was enormous. It looked more like a club, all black, the walls and ceiling removed to the exterior shell. Even the windows had been blacked out, the only light was from the glow of a few sunlight pipes coming from the roof.

"Do you live here?"

"In another area, but yes."

"What is this place?"

"Where we practise."

"Ahh...The Ministry of Harmony. Is that it?"

He nodded and motioned for me to follow.

"Doesn't look very harmonious, except its all black. Looks more like a goth club."

"A what?" he turned and asked.

Never mind. Came here to fill you in."

"You need to stay clear of the church. Told you that already, didn't I"?

Out of the blackness appeared a black cubic seating area. He dropped himself and all his legs on a cube and invited me to have a seat beside him.

"Well—" I started to explain.

"No excuses. Someone may have been seriously injured in

the sewer. The others in our team wanted to detain you, but I intervened since the most damage was done by that dog."

"Neep…his name is Neep."

"Then Neep is lucky they didn't prefer charges. That guy spent a night in hospital…three stitches, I think."

"They threatened us. Got less than they deserved. We recorded their faces too. One was the guy who chased us by the church, and we are certain it was him in Nora's house too. Neep confirmed his scent."

"Nonetheless."

"We were in a public space, Agent Rossi."

"Nonetheless."

"Understood. But we also have an intact implant, the kind they use to control people."

He must not have known that, because his body suddenly went still.

"Checking with your master?" I taunted.

"Inventory, database," he replied. "We don't have one. Are you willing to give it to us?"

"Why?"

"We have far more resources than you. We could study it and find a fix."

"Hmm."

"And everything made has provenance built-in. We could find-out who made it and where, even down to the components and software."

"Everything?"

"If there are dark parts, we'll find that out too. Now *that* may be highly illegal," Agent Rossi chuckled as though he relished the prospect."

"And what you find will be made public?"

There was a pause, then, "If you wish."

"I do. Don't want this going sideways."

"It requires trust," Rossi said, his many legs beginning to move.

"That from a spider in his hell home."

"It serves its purpose. Now do we get the implant or not?"

"Are we being recorded?"

"Of course."

"Then for the record and in the interests of promoting harmony and all that, I will try to get it for you."

"Good. It may help us with the endgame."

"Endgame?"

"We've been running simulations to encourage a harmonious result. There are a few high probability scenarios."

"There always are. Can you tell me the one preferred?"

"No, we are forbidden. It would limit your power of free choice."

"Of course," I sighed. "But manipulating us is *not* forbidden?"

"We prefer to see it as encouragement."

I shrugged, "I'm willing to take encouragement so long as the bad guys are stopped from doing further harm."

"That is our goal as well. Just be sure you and your friends don't become bad guys in pursuit of bad guys."

"Good and bad are relative terms."

"I am speaking of the law."

"I know, just pulling your legs."

"I understood that. I have something more than encouragement for you. We can assist with protecting your home if you will allow us."

"Such as?"

He walked me to the entrance before answering. "Such as special equipment that your dog friend cannot get."

"I'll get back to you on that. Some of us are sensitive to…well…to the state watching us constantly."

"It's for the common good—"

I don't need another lecture."

"Nor I your suspicions. Remember, I too am a sensitive caring human being."

I laughed, "Could've fooled me. Next time can we meet without cosplay?"

"Absolutely!"

***

It was Darwina predictably who objected to the Ministry of Harmony placing any of their security devices in "her" home. "They could turn us into zombies," she said, making Rebecca shudder.

"To what end? So, we could eat our neighbours? Doesn't sound very harmonious, does it?"

"Well maybe they could remove our memories."

I felt like banging my head on the breakfast table. Fortunately, we had a dog on hand, whose judgement was more valued than mine.

"They have good tech," Neep said through our thought implants. "Went to a conference. They showed us. Wish I could get some…like the calming mist. Not sure it works on dogs."

"See, even Neep thinks its OK." I looked at him for support, but he had already lost interest because of a squirrel which suddenly appeared at the back door.

Darwina capitulated. "Alright, alright. But this had better be it, or I'm leaving."

I might too, I thought as I contacted Agent Rossi.

***

I had never been here before. Just heard about it from his sister Rebecca. It was downtown, overlooking the river. Very posh and stuffed with European antiques, mostly British from the nineteenth century.

Tattie did not mind handing over the church implant. In fact, he was relieved to be free of it and the responsibility of preserving it for us. "I worry it has tracking imbedded," he said to me as we drank some spiked coffee in his apartment. "We couldn't determine that. It was safe enough having it at work. We have great security there. Not so much here."

I thought about what he said. Most devices like this had locators or trackers and bringing it home could be as hazardous as painting a bull's eyes on our back.

"My sister concerns me more," he continued.

"How so?" I asked, anticipating the answer.

"Umm…that girl…Darwina."

"Yes, I know she's a lesbian."

Tatties eyebrows shot up. "I suspected…but."

"And yes, she and Rebecca are a couple, if that's what you're trying to ask."

"I see. Never thought…"

"It's OK, they seem happy enough."

"Maybe it's a stage?"

I shrugged.

"She had boyfriends; you know."

"Does it bother you?"

"Only that…I thought we were close, yet I didn't know, and she didn't tell me."

"Life is like that. Keep loving each other and all will be well."

He smiled.

"Just curious. Who was your friend who gave you the implant?"

He smiled again. "I'm glad this went no further. When I told her what this was about, she wanted to go back in and collect evidence!"

I looked at him, at his eyes crinkling and glistening as he told me about her. It was love. "How did you meet?"

"Oh, she works here. She's one of the lab techs who prepares your treatments."

"And she's the one who dissected her implant?"

"Yes, under my guidance of course."

"Obviously. I hope I meet her soon. I need to thank her."

By the grin stuck on Tattie's face that must have pleased him. Then he surprised me. "How are you and Nora doing?"

"There is no me and Nora. She has a boyfriend."

Tattie's face went from happy grin to perplexed. "Oh…sorry," he mumbled.

"It was a delusional fantasy. I'm a hundred years older. It would never work."

"There are lots of single women your age," Tattie said, no doubt trying to be encouraging.

"Yes, but they've lived so long, they think they know everything, and they are insufferable."

"Same as the men."

"Yep."

"No one thought of that when they started selling this stuff."

"Unintended consequences."

The conversation was becoming depressing, so I was thankful when he changed the subject.

"Rebecca wants to celebrate Christmas at our farm and invite everyone."

"Oh, how nice!"

"And I hope to introduce Geetika to everyone."

"Including Rebecca?"

"Umm, yes."

"You too are a pair," I laughed.

"I suppose we are. Our parents held their cards close to their chest, too."

"The apple doesn't fall far from the tree," I said, quoting another ancient.

***

I was happy for Tattie. It explained his reticence to be involved. I think at this point all of us were feeling much the same. We needed an endgame, as Rossi called it. And the sooner the better.

"A smelly government guy came by and installed something while you were away," Darwina said, shouting at me from the kitchen when I returned.

"Any instructions?" I shouted back, removing my boots.

Darwina came toward me, a swagger in her step.

"If attacked, stay away from windows and doors."

"Great, that's helpful," I said.

"Well Neep seemed pleased. He inspected the work and gave it a seal of approval."

"He peed on it?"

"Yep."

I looked at her, trying to decide what I had failed to notice. It was the hair again. This time trimmed short and with a metallic finish that made her look like she was wearing a wire helmet. "Upgrade?" I asked.

"The latest. It blocks unwanted signals."

"Such as?"

"Such as someone trying to control my mind."

"God forbid that. But it is fetching in a military-industrial way."

She grinned, approving my comment.

"I need some coffee," I said, brushing past her.

"You'll have to make it. I don't do cooking anymore and Rebecca is busy knitting."

"Nice to hear. You're a proper family."

Rebecca had re-organized the kitchen, and now nothing could be found without resorting to the digital map. I sighed and wondered if this is what it is like to lose one's home. Familiarity brings comfort and contentment. Her well-intended efforts providing confusion and upset, for me at least. But it was as much my fault because I refused to use the digital search feature, on principle. So, I was reduced to opening many cupboards and drawers, with Darwina leaning on the door jamb shaking her head in disgust. It took me longer, but I did find the ingredients in due course, then turned and gave her the finger. She laughed and said something derogatory about codgers.

The coffee was worth the hassle and I made enough for the three of us then sat at the kitchen table facing the sliding back door, wondering what had happened to that squirrel. My mind gainfully occupied, I was surprised when Rebecca came up behind me, gave me a hug and asked for forgiveness for messing up my kitchen. She is such a sweet thing that I had to lie and say it was a big improvement, long overdo, and thanked her all her hard work, so on. Such is the life of a rider. When we mess up or hurt feelings, we must live with the consequences for an extremely long time.

Meanwhile, Darwina had been watching us from the other end of the table and returned my finger gesture with a chuckle. She seemed to understand me the best, except perhaps Neep whose job was to study humans.

"How is my dear brother?" Rebecca said when she came back with her coffee.

"He is doing well. Gave me this thing." I took the plastic box holding the church implant out of my pocket and placed it on the table for all to see.

They both stared at it like it was a wonder of the world.

"I want to give it to Rossi."

"It's intact?" Darwina asked.

"Yep, but for the bit they disabled." I said trying not to reveal too much openly.

Darwina looked anxious. "Get it out of here, Amir. It's dangerous."

"I will. Already contacted Rossi. He should be here soon. More news. Turns out the good Doctor Tattie has a girl-friend." I said that watching Rebecca's reaction. It was a happy nod. "You know?" I asked her.

"Yes, she's his lab tech. He thinks I don't notice anything."

I laughed. "He seems happier than I've seen him...well...ever."

"Yes! Me too." Rebecca said looking at Darwina with love. I sighed.

***

The strikingly handsome man at the door was Special Agent Tony Rossi, simply dressed in what they call "service practical" which to me looks like glorified surgery scrubs encased in an environmentally controlled overalls-coat. Rebecca greeted him at the door, and I noticed a blush as she stammered and helped him remove the coat. Yes, he was that handsome, with wavy black hair, olive skin and a strong hooked nose from his heritage. But it was his wide, expressive mouth and sparkling white teeth which first drew the eye. It is no wonder he preferred cosplay. Otherwise, the ladies, and no doubt some men, otherwise would be distracted from his purpose.

"The real Tony Rossi," I grinned on inviting him to join us in the living room. I pointed him to Nora's Poang chair, for a laugh.

"You live comfortably," he said after a cursory look.

Rebecca ran back to the safety of the kitchen. Darwina, having noticed Rebecca's reaction to him, glared from her perch on the sofa.

Rossi nodded at her and said, "Darwina, nice to see you again."

Darwina deepened her scowl and I was beginning to wish Rossi had come as a teddy bear.

"I heard your man was here and did an installation."

Rossi nodded.

"Been thinking. I invited you to give you something, but it might be to mutual advantage if we kept it a few more days."

Rossi cocked his head and smiled. I explained my cunning plan. He laughed and slapped his knee. Even Darwina laughed at the image of it. "It could work," he said, "but no violence, and stow that dagger, Darwina."

She gave him the finger. I sighed. Then Nora arrived, complaining about the late deliver of building supplies. I waited as she removed her coat. She came in, headed for her Poang chair, and as if on cue, he rose to meet her, his smile dazzling, his visage god-like, his hand extended in loving greeting. She stopped, stunned, her eyes went wide, her face flushed, and she blurted, "Tony?"

He embraced her, whispered something in her ear. She turned to us, her blush deepening and said, "Meet my new boyfriend, Tony Rossi."

***

I was surprised it took them so long to arrive. The same stupid duo, the Hungarian fellow, and his pal, easily seen peering through my sliding back door. The night was blustery with bands of sleet tickling the siding. And we had done as instructed and positioned ourselves away from doors and windows, wrapped in blankets for the wait. Neep had licked us awake when the perimeter was breached. I glanced back from the nefarious pair at the door to my friends. Darwina was in a shadow by the wall with her hoe. Rebecca, Nora, and Neep were behind the sofa. I was closest to our intruders, in the kitchen several feet away from them, prepared to flip the light switch.

They were prying the lock. If they got in unopposed, we would be trapped. It was an unsettling feeling. There was a snap, metal and wood breaking, then some muffled whispers. I stopped breathing to listen. I knew the sound that back door made when it slid on its track. I wanted to confront them as soon as they entered. It would be a violation of my space, and I hated that. But Rossi had advised we wait. I prayed he knew what he was doing.

The door opened slowly, they must have pushed something through the opening to see if it set-off alarms, because I heard one of them whisper, "Clear."

I heard the door inching open. Neep uttered a low growl. Nora shushed him. I normally had a wooden security bar to prevent the door sliding open too far. Rossi had told me to remove it as well as other security. "We want this to be easy for them," he had said with a wink.

I heard the door open more. Did they not stop and wonder why entry as so easy? What fools! I tensed, ready to confront them. I heard Nora stifle a sneeze.

I peaked out from my hiding place. A large dark shape was slithering through the entrance, the sleet following him. *Wait*, I reminded myself. *Rossi said to wait. But for what?*

The dark shape turned. His partly covered face caught some light. The Hungarian. He turned to his partner and flicked his chin. The other man slid through the opening, his extra bulk catching the broken lock making him swear. I waited, the fear rising in my belly.

And then it happened as the Hungarian took the first step toward me. Something sizzled and they stopped. I watched. There was not a sound nor movement from them. I jumped up and turned on the lights. There they were frozen like statues carved in mid-step. I laughed. They did not.

Nora let go of Neep when the front door rang. It was Special Agent Rossi and the local policewoman.

"Hah! What do we have here?" Rossi said, dressed as a crow again.

"You got here fast," I said.

"We tracked them from the church compound. We were waiting outside," he explained.

"Hmm. How did we do as tethered goats?" I said with more than a hint of sarcasm.

"Oh, very well actually, and I knew you would want to keep the implant to trap them," he chuckled. "Couldn't resist, could you?"

"I suppose not," I sighed.

"We used a localized disharmony field. Completely blocks synapses." Rossi said to Nora who had asked. While Rossi was gloating, the policewoman placed restraints on our intruders then released the field. They slumped, boneless to the floor, then begged for mercy. It must have been a frightening experience, immobilized yet conscious. I had little empathy for them. They were pawns like us, and no doubt controlled by implants, but we all have some level of control, don't we? And for that I could not forgive them. But Rebecca's heart was not as hard as mine. She was busy making tea and cookies to share, including with the perps who she treated as special guests. Meanwhile, the policewoman worked efficiently, scanning their health, and giving them calming scent while lovingly telling them repeatedly that all will be well.

"These guys have those church implants. Feel sorry for them. Not sure they are in complete control of their actions," Rossi confirmed to Nora who had sidled up to him.

"So, they likely won't be charged with anything," I said.

"If they cooperate, and they likely will once we remove the implants."

Nora was smiling at her new hero. Rossi and the policewoman had things well in hand, and we had given over everything we could, including our church implant.

I went to the living room to check on Darwina.

"Damn, I was hoping for more action than that," Darwina whispered.

"Sorry, but this was a setup."

"I gathered that. But would've been nice to have let me and Neep at them for a few seconds…as a reward." I could see her grimacing in the dim light, her curly steel helmet glowing in frustrated anger.

"Come here you," I said understanding her unrequited frustration.

I opened my arms, and for some reason, and for the first time, she gave me a warm hug and whispered, "Thank you for tolerating me."

***

Later that morning, Rossi notified us that our intruders were cooperating and had offered up a lot of information about the church and the group responsible for the transgressions.

Nora and Darwina had also given Rossi everything they had gathered on Kevin Nguyen and his company and what they were up to in Divine Life. That and the information encoded in the illegal implants lead us to assume the case was solved and soon there would be a public announcement of arrests. But it was not to be as we found out later that day on receiving a Cease-and-Desist order, delivered in person by an officious prig who claimed to be an Officer of the Regional Court. The church had decided to fight back.

| 12 |

Chapter Twelve

According to Special Agent Rossi, the intent of the Justice AI was to provide a cooling off period, and they decided this based on the documented bruises sustained by the church henchmen while in a public space, namely the sewer near their compound. That was fine with me, since their men were in custody and we also obtained a ten-day Cease-and-Desist against the church. It was a stand-off to preserve harmony. That gave me time to find Ranjit and Lei without having to worry about being ambushed by hostile churchgoers.

I had no luck contacting my former friends using normal methods, and I had been to Ranjit's old apartment, the one with the VR interior. The building AI told me there was no one by that name in residence but I knew some people liked to remain hidden, so I could not depend completely on that. So, I went to the university building complex again, looking for Zhang Lei.

He looked like a corpse in his white shroud and powdered

head, shaven clean. He blinked then cursed when he saw me. "May I come in?" I asked.

"If you must," he answered, but did not step aside till I took a step toward him.

His pod was the same as I remembered, but for the litter of decomposing delivery food remains.

"Are you alright," I said, feeling sorry for him.

"Oh...ahh yes. Working on a project in DL, night and day." He slumped on the edge of his DL cradle, his body deflating.

"You need to get out more. You are beginning to look ill."

He scrunched his face. "If you're looking for Ranjit, I won't tell you."

I looked about for any sign that Ranjit had been there. There was nothing. "What are you working on in DL"

That did get a reaction. He opened his mouth to speak then shut it.

"Remember what happened last time? Do you want a repeat?"

"That was cruel and unnecessary," Lei said, angry eyes on me.

"I think you are working on something with Ranjit in DL using my credits, perhaps a large, expensive project."

The ire grew on his face. I had to be careful. Lei was capable of anything.

"Alright, I'll leave you in peace. Convey my greetings to Ranjit and tell him I may have a way for him to make a lot of credits and pay back what he owes me."

I was not sure he heard because he turned away and muttered. I waited a moment. He muttered again, then turned and said, "He's at the senior's centre."

***

"They were going to kill me, I had no choice," Ranjit pleaded. Of course, he was lying. The only one who might want to kill him was me and surely, he knew I would not go that far. But he seldom failed to be amusing and outrageous and for that I found myself pulled back to his world. A curious character flaw on my part considering what he had done to me.

He was renting one of the short-term rooms at the centre, paying by the day and renting the Divine Life cradle by the hour. It was a pathetic existence for someone who once had a good job in government service, all apparently wasted on crazy lovers and mad schemes.

"I still want my money back, you know."

Ranjit shook his head seeming as pained as I felt at the loss of my savings. "It's been put to good use. You will see. Why don't you join us in DL? We would make a fab team!" he said as though he meant it.

"I prefer reality."

"Welcome to reality," he said, wide armed and laughing amid the austerity.

"What happened in India? Why did you come back?"

Strangely, Ranjit was wearing a cheap nondescript outfit typical of a tradesman. And he did not answer until I told him forcefully that I needed to know.

"Umm…ahh…a spot of trouble is all."

"Such as?"

He sighed. "Oh Amir, life is like sailing a sea of sharks in foul weather."

"You were swindled, weren't you?"

"It was my family!"

I was not sure if it was another of his lies, but his face seemed to show real anguish, down to the telltale runny nose. Regardless, I would use him. "You still owe me, and I don't care how you spent or lost my credits. If you intend to live in this region, I will have recompense."

He nodded. I think he understood my resolve because he asked, "What must I do?"

***

We were missing them all. Nora had not been over in a few days, evidently obsessed with her new boyfriend, and Rebecca and her brother had escaped to their farm for some family bonding and to prepare for Christmas. That left Darwina, Neep and I to get on each other's nerves.

"Have you heard anything from the Ministry of Justice?" Darwina asked for the third time since breakfast.

"No, have you?" I tried to turn it back on her.

"They said they would contact you. Is your memory failing?" She was at the sink washing dishes, her least favourite task, but it was her turn now that our housewife was absent.

"My memory is not the issue. It's your constant nagging. I'll let you know if there's news." Neep seemed to be laughing at us as he watched from his spot on the floor, his chin resting on a plush toy.

Darwina said something unkind under her breath. I decided to leave before pettiness escalated to stupidity, then regret. But Darwina was right. We had heard nothing from the government in several days and it was becoming worrisome, like when you go for a medical test and they do not call back with the results. I was tugging on my winter boots when Neep said, "Join you for a walk?"

"Not going far, it looks slippery out there. Just want to clear my head."

"Me too," he replied.

The sidewalk had been treated but the rest of our neighbourhood was an icy mess of coated branches and spikey grass. My boots sensed the lack of traction and instantly increased grip. Today I was appreciative of our nanny tech that kept us comfortable and safe. Other days I cursed it, like the time I tried to clean my coat only to find that as soon as I touched it with water, the repellant feature turned on. It took me half-an hour of searching the manual and going through several layers of menus to be able to disable the damned thing so I could sponge off some spots.

Neep was a good partner for a walk. He said little, absorbed in his world of sounds and smells. That is until he decided to drag me to a pile of snow in front of the house next door. I assumed he wanted a pee, so I let him lead. But instead of peeing, he dug.

What he revealed was a ball. It appeared to be a tennis ball. I laughed and said, "Good boy! Want to chase it?"

Neep barked and sent me a thought, "No stupid, look inside...not tennis, electronics."

Back home, Darwina was able to cut it open. Neep was right. It was full of something electronic. "It's transmitting," Neep said.

"What?" I asked, hoping he knew.

"Encrypted. Call police."

***

With exemplary efficiency, the policewoman took our statement and the evidence. Special Agent Rossi arrived minutes later, sans cosplay outfit. He had been with Nora, helping her choose wall colours or some such domestic nonsense. "Would placing a surveillance device be a breach of the Cease-and-Desist order?" I asked.

"Of course, it would. They are spying on us," Darwina opined as though she were an expert.

Rossi was communicating with someone, his head tilted, finger in his ear, ignoring our discussion.

Darwina let Nora in. She looked especially radiant. *Love must be good for her,* I thought, recalling the feeling. "I need coffee," Nora said.

"Darwina just made some," I answered.

We both watched her slowly walk down the hall to the kitchen. She looked like she had just run a marathon. "I'll bet she's been up all night," Darwina said, smirking.

I am not sure why but the sight of Nora, wrapped in a thick sweater and wearing hand knit slippers, reminded me of something. That image linked in my brain with one much older. Perhaps my mother in those bad old days, or was it my wife, or maybe a collage of images? And I perceived that the now would become not much more than that: ephemeral, half-remembered memories, like the life my wife and I shared, long ago. I realized I was attached to that which I could barely recollect now, only kept alive through imperfect repetition.

"They will be cautioned," Rossi said finally after consulting the Ministry. "It's a minor breach," he added.

"Minor?" Darwina blurted.

"We are going with that, yes. The church found your device too…yesterday…and then tit-for-tat and here we are."

"Ahh," I said.

Darwina grumbled. Nora returned; her nose stuck in the steam coming off her cup. "What's up?" she asked.

Rossi explained it again for her benefit, then added that he had just been informed that other charges were being filed as he was speaking.

"Who?" I asked.

"Umm…Kevin Nguyen…for manufacturing illegal tech," Rossi looked at Nora and mouthed, "Sorry."

"No one else?" Darwina interrupted.

But Rossi did not answer her and instead made his apologies and left.

"I may have to testify. This could go on for years," Nora sighed then nested in her Poang chair.

"Is this the end?" Darwina asked.

***

It was not the end. But it was highly satisfying seeing news vids of Kevin's lab being closed and Kevin named as one of those detained and charged. One small victory for mankind. But it did not satisfy completely, so next day I contacted Rossi again. His response was short: I was becoming a nuisance and if there was any news, he would contact me. I other words, do not call me, I'll call you, and said in a way that he might not, purely out of pique. I briefly considered destroying his relationship with Nora before anger settled to resentment. We must wait. No way around it. But there was the remaining question about the library and the suggestion that the archives might be hidden somewhere in the church compound. We had recordings to indicate such and suggestions from the Imam to indicate the reason for their theft. But how do we get in and verify it? We needed concrete proof for the authorities to act. Second-hand info would not cut it. And that is why I reluctantly contacted Doctor Tattie.

"We are not in Guelph," Tattie said.

"I know. I'm sorry to disturb you but things are coming to a head and there seems no other way."

"We don't have the implant, so it won't work, Amir. And it's too dangerous, so forget it."

"What if we could get the implant back?" I said, combing my mind for a solution.

"Highly unlikely, and even if you could get it, I won't allow her to use it. She might get killed, Amir. No, I won't allow it! And furthermore—"

It was interesting to experience a forceful Tattie. The power of love made real. But I had no patience for his atypical behaviour. "I hear you, Tattie. Please stop and think about how you *can* help us. These are desperate times. We *need* you!" I knew he liked being needed. It was part of the reason he had become a doctor, as well as the top pay, of course.

"Can you really get the implant, back?"

"Yes," I said confidently, lying through my teeth.

"Hmm. I can send you a pic of my friend. She looks a bit like Darwina…but prettier and with long hair, and—"

"And if we made them look more alike and used your girlfriend's implant…Hah!"

"Send the pic, Tattie and thank you…but please ask her permission first."

"I will, but she wants this resolved too, so our lives can…"

I was already hollering down the stairs for Darwina.

***

I knew Darwina would do it. I just had to get the church implant back from the authorities. I called Rossi. No answer, no call-back. This one would have to be on Nora, and we had to meet in her favourite place, the sewer.

"Are you two insane?" Nora exploded on hearing our half-baked plan.

"It's the only way. The government won't raid a church without absolute proof," I pleaded. "And besides, we all want closure, and this will provide it."

"They have Kevin. That's enough closure for me."

She stood there in the sewer, defiant. I had to find another approach. "Why not just put our proposition before Special Agent Tony, and let him decide? No harm in that, surely?"

"Except, he'll think I'm as crazy as you two. Have you forgotten the Cease-and-Desist order?"

"It expires in four days. We can act after that," Darwina said.

Nora shook her head. "It won't work. That church implant is coded for Tattie's girlfriend. Even if Darwina tries to look like her, it won't matter. Their men were captured while trying to retrieve it. Don't you see? It will be on a hotlist and as soon as it crosses their perimeter, Darwina will be caught."

"Agreed," Darwina and I said at once.

Nora glared at us both, sighed then asked, "OK, what is the rest of your plan and why do you need me?"

"Simple," I said. "Once we get the implant back, we hack it and change the ID code."

Nora laughed, then said our idea confirmed her suspicions that we were missing a few vital mental parts. But in the end, she agreed to help, provided we were honest with Tony.

"That will be the easy part," I said with a wink.

"Sure. Let's get out of here. And I get to pick the locale of our next meeting."

"I know a really nice sewer in the east end," Darwina chuckled.

***

His apartment was better than a sewer, but not much. Rossi guided us through a labyrinth he had recently constructed to the almost invisible seating area we had used before. I watched the women's expressions as we sat. Darwina looked like she had a day pass to heaven. Nora, the opposite. She looked appalled. "This could be your new home," I teased.

To make matters worse, Rossi was in his evil crow cosplay that did not at all match the words offered lovingly to Nora. Should I tell him, she hated creepy places and ugly men? Nah.

Polite greetings over we got down to business. I repeated everything we had told Nora in the sewer and waited for his objections. There were none. Instead, he paced before us, fussing with his wing feathers. He was really getting good at this cosplay, down to using crow mannerisms. I asked if he had any issues with our plan. He cawed, "Not yet. Wait."

I looked at the women and smiled my encouragement. A few more caws and feather flaps and he stopped, then seemed to read his response as though it were a lecture. He started with the usual dire warnings and reminders to maintain harmony and refrain from breaking the law.

"Is it a yes or a no?" I said interrupting.

"Wait. I must transmit this to you, so it is on the record."

"I take that as a yes, that you will help."

Nora glared at me. Rossi sighed and continued his speech which included several more boring caveats. I was about to fall into stupor when he said, "...it has been investigated and there is no proof of who or what caused the burning of the library. Furthermore, we have no solid proof of the existence of the library archives in the church compound."

I rolled my eyes. "We already know this—"

I thought I saw a crow smirk, "Yes...thank you for confirming it. Any questions from the ladies?"

They shook their heads. Rossi continued, "Here is the part you may not know. The two men captured at your house are cooperating, and after extensive truth testing, we know that neither were involved in the burning of the library nor the theft of archives. We assumed it was them and could wrap this case up quickly, but—"

"Someone else did it?" I blurted.

"Seems so," Rossi answered.

Silence accompanied the blackness between us. Then Rossi cleared his throat and told us what we were about to hear must remain a secret. We agreed. I felt like a schoolboy after class doing something illicit behind the bleachers with my chums. Too many secrets. Their weight may sink us in the end. That is what I was thinking anyway when Rossi told us that Kevin Nguyen was cooperating and ready to help.

Nora spoke next. "Ask him if there is a back-door to the implant, so we can change ID codes."

***

"A watched pot never boils." I remember a woman telling me that when I was a boy, and it was never so apt as now. The four days till our Cease-and-Desist order was to expire seemed to take for ever, even though we tried to stay busy. Our plan was to not plan, until we had the modified church implant in hand, and we were free of the order. We did not want to give anyone time to plan countermeasures. It would be a quick hack and dash, get what we could and flee. That was the idea, anyway. But the lack of planning was worrisome and ate away at my self-confidence. Those four days were hellish, yet nothing happened till Darwina bounced in, her coat dotted with fresh snow. "Been downtown. Good to see my friends," she said in an emphatic voice which suggested she had something important to say.

"Your brat friends?" I asked.

"The same," she answered, getting my coat from the closet.

"I'm going to take Neep for a walk, like to join us, maybe Nora would like a break too."

"Be delighted."

It was a walk to nowhere. Large flakes of wet snow were drifting down, the kind that could be caught on your tongue when you stuck it out. We were on a trail at the neighbourhood park. A few others were about. Mothers with buggies filled with more gear than needed for a space mission, and alongside a small child over-dressed and tripping constantly as a result. We could consult briefly here. It was not as good as a sewer, but Nora had refused another one there a few days ago and we did not want anymore needless drama.

Darwina blew into her mittens. "My friends in DL want more credits."

"Sounds like extortion," I said.

"No. Just credits for services rendered. They gave it to me without payment. We might regret it if they get nothing in return and we need them again."

"Alright, but how much?"

"Doesn't matter, I'll pay," Nora said. "Tell us what they found."

"This is good. Come close, we all need a big hug, don't we Neep."

So, there we were, on a snowy trail, the three of us in a huddle, Neep in the middle looking up at our faces pressed together. Darwina giggled and whispered, "Can't trust this to thought comms. But the church is in DL, at least some of them, and they are part religious, part political. They are trying to get converts in DL."

"Our laws don't apply there. DL is international and exempt," Nora explained.

Darwina continued. "Yes, and my friends compiled a list of their avatar names and compared them with Tattie's list descriptions. They were surprisingly easy to match up."

"Humans are conceited creatures. We tend to make our avatars look like our real selves," noted Nora, but of course we all knew that.

I smiled. "Thank your friends, Darwina, and I'll contribute more credits for them. I think I may have a way to use that info, but not right now. Let's keep this between us, no sense alerting anyone, right Nora?"

"I won't tell Tony, if that's what you're implying," Nora said.

"And that includes you Neep," I laughed and gave him a playful nudge with my boot. Our consultation hug in the park over, I fished a ball out of my pocket and threw it as far as I could. Neep was off in a fury of snow and barks to retrieve it.

***

The day had arrived. We were officially free, and first thing that morning graced by a visit from Special Agent Rossi with Nora trailing close behind.

"Don't ask," was the first thing he said, brushing past me at the door like he owned the place. We had finished breakfast, but he targeted the last of the coffee, swiftly poured himself a mug and slugged it down before inviting us to the living room.

"Remember my warnings," Rossi started. "Here it is, reprogrammed as an admin ID. Should get you in anywhere." He slid it across the coffee table toward me. "This could get me in a heap of bother. Don't let me down."

With that, he turned, gave Nora a peck on the cheek and left.

Darwina had been silent till now. "Give it to me Amir. I'll go in."

I shook my head and placed the tiny plastic box in my pocket. "You've taken too many risks. I'll do it. All the elders in the church are men. With this ID, they will be looking for an older man, not a young woman."

Darwina was about to say something, likely derogatory

about codgers, when Nora spoke up, "I'm going in. I started this mess and I'll finish it."

None of us were willing to concede.

Then Nora said, "Amir is right, that ID matches him best. And Darwina clearly doesn't belong there."

That was not very diplomatic, but the truth. "It's settled then," I said.

Darwina rolled her eyes. Nora disagreed. "It's not settled. I have one as well." She pulled a small box out of the folds of her sweater and slapped it on the table. I stared at it wondering. "That's Tattie's, the one we took out of his back and stomped."

"What the?" Darwina exclaimed.

Nora grinned. "I took it to work and one of the techs fixed it. It's reprogrammable now too."

Darwina stuck out her hand. "Give it to me. You two are incompetent in a fight."

Nora and I took exception. I reminded her that I was the one who took down the two church henchmen, and Nora suggested in impolite terms that the project needed a leader with intelligence and finesse. It was about to turn into a verbal brawl, when Neep, who had been snoozing, barked, and sent us a thought that we should all go in a coordinated raid which included him.

We looked at each other. He was right. We nodded and thanked the little dog who managed to do what we humans could not. Unite us.

"Let's get planning," Darwina said, unrolling a flexi-screen map on the coffee table.

***

It was late afternoon next day; a time Tattie had told us the church compound was least busy yet open to the public. We were readying ourselves. I had searched my closet and found an outfit I had worn when I was a working scientist. It still looked presentable provided one did not look too closely. I looked in the mirror and smiled at my old self. I was to play the role of church elder with my hacked implant. After further skirmishes with Darwina and Nora, it was decided I was the logical choice, with Nora as back-up and Darwina and Neep providing distraction and cover.

In his ass-covering lectures, Rossi had repeated that I must give the implant back to Tattie's girlfriend as-soon-as, since that was the excuse used to have it released from the Ministry of Justice storage. I agreed. Rossi had also mentioned that hacking illegal tech was not illegal. At least that conundrum should confound the Justice AI, at any rate. His opinion, not mine. But I did not want to be the one testing it. We were being setup as the fall guys again should anything go wrong. We all knew it, and agreed to participate, nonetheless. Stupid us.

"You look like someone's grandfather in that," Darwina laughingly said when I met them in the kitchen.

"Thanks. I was expecting great-grandfather."

Darwina and Neep were wearing matching camo outfits, pockets stuffed with gear. "Going on a survivalist outing?" I asked.

"We mean to do more than survive. We mean to thrive and come back alive," Darwina shot back a saying current among her group.

The previous evening, we had formulated our plan of attack. It was pure Darwina with no thought of adverse consequences. I had my own back-up plan, having lived through one too many personal disasters.

Nora came charging down from upstairs, almost tripping over Neep whose camo was proving highly effective. Her hair was tied up, no digital makeup, and dressed in the ugliest pair of coveralls imaginable. Nora noticed my disapproving stare and said, "Borrowed these from Tony," as though that explained it. Nora would be using Tattie's old implant, re-assigned with the identity of one of the church maintenance women. She was passable, assuming she did not linger or stop to chat with the locals.

We were ready, sort of, and were going over the plan once again, when Tattie, Rebecca, and Tattie's girlfriend Geetika unexpectedly arrived.

"The Cease-and-Desist is up and we thought you might have something planned," Tattie said with an expectant air about him.

"It'll be a party." I jested.

"Hmm. By appearances, perhaps more," he said, careful not to say too much openly.

"You guys can help," Darwina said after giving Rebecca a brief hug and welcome.

"How so?" Tattie prompted.

Darwina explained, "Well, Rebecca can make supper and hold down the fort and you and...ahh...Geetika can help with transportation. You know how those auto-cabs hate to wait without a paying customer."

"Consider it done. Now when will this party begin?" Tattie asked.

"Now," I said. "It starts now. We were about to leave when you arrived."

***

Darwina and Neep went first, taking the sewer leading to the church compound. They would try to draw security away while we waltzed in bold as brass and documented the presence of the library archives, before making our valiant escape. That was our expectation, however naive. Nora had perfected her system of word codes that we could use over regular thought comms. It would be enough to confuse them for a while, she had explained. We had spent the previous evening memorizing them, while I, a firm believer in belt and suspenders, wrote the important words on my wrist.

Nora and I were taken to the entrance of the church compound. Tattie would stay with the car with Geetika. It was late afternoon, the sun low in the late chill sky, hidden by grey clouds. The weather forecast called for a dusting of snow by morning. The solstice was rapidly approaching and along with it the promise of renewal and spring. It was what we yearned for, an end to this insanity and a happy new life free of worries. But it was that yearning which worried me most as Nora disembarked and waved to Tattie. Yearning often as not leads to disaster. It makes one reckless, imprudent, and willing to throw the dice to risk all on one throw. Desire makes us weak and foolish, yet here we were, walking into the lion's den with nothing to gain but the satisfaction of bringing a few unimportant locals to justice, and everything to lose should we fail. An intelligent species would err on the side of self-preservation, but not us. My mind in torment, I watched Nora trudge up the hill toward the church, lunch bag in hand. I wished her well. I would be next.

"No one here," Darwina said by thought message. "It's weird."

"Stay the course and be vigilant. They may have a few surprises," I thought back to her.

"Yeah, but Neep is picking up nothing."

"Alright but pull back if you are opposed."

"Yep, we'll draw them away if we can."

That was the last I heard from them before Tattie let me out onto the street, the chill piercing my ancient, unheated overcoat. *Be calm*, I said to myself. *Exude confidence and normalcy.* Funny how we think doing that might alter results in a day when everyone is monitored constantly, and outward appearances easily penetrated. Regardless, I followed Nora's path toward the main admin building located to the right of what was once the parking lot.

I bathed myself in a cloud of frosty steam as I walked, hoping beyond hope that it would obscure my face. I had his identity code in my implant but looked nothing like him, the church admin. Should I run into one of his friends, the ruse would be up, and if the door security required a body scan, same thing. There was no one about. It was surprisingly deserted, and the closer I got, the more my mind gasped for air in that sea of doubt. How could this possibly work? We should not have listened to Darwina. This would not easy, nor likely to succeed. I saw Nora enter the admin building. Nothing stopped her. At least we could get out of the cold, but into what? It felt like a trap.

Nora said in code, "I'm in. No one here."

I reached the entrance door, took a deep breath, and pulled it open. Nora was nowhere to be seen.

"Keep going...quickly," she said.

I mentally consulted Tattie's crude map. *Take the stairs at the end of the hall down to the basement,* I reminded myself.

I walked past the maintenance room. Nora was there, waiting. She dipped her head as I passed. It was not far now, the locked storage room. And there it was, 16a, Church Archives, it said on the sign. I looked back down the hall. There was no one. I listened. Not a sound but for the ticking and swooshing of heating pipes over my head. I told the door to open. The lights came on and I was greeted by the smell of old paper and plastic. I was fully expecting to be enveloped in a cunning trap when I entered. But there was nothing but a room with rows of metal shelves filled with filing boxes, a tidy desk off to the left, and directly in front on the floor, a stack of cartons clearly labelled "Library Archives".

"This is too easy," I mused. I sent a coded thought to Nora, Darwina and Neep that I was in and had located the archive. I turned on record and opened a box filled with plastic microfiches. I opened a few more. Same thing. I pulled out a microfiche and held it up to the light, recording constantly. Someone had written on it: Guelph Public Library,1998. I replaced it and opened several more boxes. There were thousands of microfiches. The scent of paranoia filled my mind. Panic followed. *This must be a trap and I the mouse,* I said to myself. I had enough proof and no doubt they did too. I was here, my image, voice, smell, and DNA. They had me. I cursed and fled back down the hall, stopping at the maintenance room to retrieve Nora and tell Darwina and Neep to clear out.

Back on the street we were greeted by a few people passing by. One said, "Thank you for visiting, please come back again," in a voice untainted by sarcasm.

It was growing dark. We hurried back down the hill. The cab was there, welcoming lights glowing from within. I almost broke into a run I was so relieved. The door slid open. A voice said, "Get in." Nora was right behind me, breathless. I ducked my head and slid in beside the shape I assumed was Tattie. I extended a hand to help Nora. The door closed and the car moved forward.

"Well done," the voice beside me said. Rossi. "I sent Tattie and Geetika home. Forgive me. We need to talk...alone, the four of us."

Four? My eyes adjusted. Imam Zia was sitting across from me, a deceptively sweet smile disguising his face.

"We were setup, weren't we?" I said to them.

"I just found out this morning," Rossi replied.

"What?" Nora asked, leaning forward, touching his knee with her hand.

Rossi returned her touch. "They made a deal last night...the Ministry and the church people."

I looked at him, his strong face showing no signs of deceit. "Then why did you let us do this?"

Rossi glanced at Imam Zia. "They...they did. I suppose they wanted insurance...proof, before consummating the agreement."

Imam Zia turned to me, "Amir, my good friend, it was managed as well as—"

"We were used, weren't we?" I asked, voicing experience-induced paranoia.

Rossi made a noise which sounded like a low growl, then said, his voice controlled, "It's not like that. We care about you. The Ministry of Justice and Reconciliation took this case out of the hands of the AI to protect all involved. This was a human decision. They knew your group was determined to resolve this and the church equally determined to fight. They let both sides try for a time, that's all. No harm done."

If I had not been so relieved, I would be angry. But the adrenaline had sapped me, and I had little fight left, "No harm? May I remind you both—" I weakly objected.

"Evidently the church will be reformed, and all will be made right. And we will help them." Imam Zia said, as though all of this were a perfect gift from an all-knowing God.

"Are you implying no charges will be laid?" I asked, my stomach souring.

"Not up to me, but I assume so," Rossi said to me while staring at Nora.

I wanted to utter a profanity, to curse whoever was the guiding hand pulling the strings of our lives. But I could not do it in front of Nora. Instead, I grumbled, "Great, and what about us?"

"You won't be charged either." Rossi answered, then waited for my attack.

But instead, I sighed. It was all a game as is much of life. I glanced over at Nora, her angry eyes were fixed on Rossi, her hands clenched. Not a good sign. Minutes later, they dropped us off at home. Nora fell into my arms and sobbed.

***

I waited a week for emotions to cool. Rebecca had mothered us to acceptance. "We are yet alive," she had told us repeatedly after a well-appreciated hug. The news had reported nothing of our adventure but for the ongoing prosecution of Kevin and his associates for producing illegal tech. The authorities could not abide that offence, apparently. As for the church, nothing was mentioned. Harmony had won out over justice. We had been warned, hadn't we? And that was why I was sitting outside in the freezing cold drinking a rapidly cooling coffee.

"You must truly love this coffee," Ranjit said, descending his voluminous self onto the chair opposite.

"The ambiance is worth it," I replied. I studied Ranjit's face, his improbable moustache, and rotund features seemingly impervious to change. We had such a long history as friends, ended in the betrayal of greed.

"I won't order," he said, in case I cared.

I shrugged.

"Are you well, Amir?" he asked, his old self which had forged our friendship appearing unexpectedly.

"I am, and you?"

"So, so."

Our eyes met. I sensed something, perhaps that grief one feels on realizing what has been lost for little gain. At least that is what I wanted him to be thinking. It was over between us, beyond using each other for mutual gain. I am sure he knew it too. I had summoned him for profit, nothing more, and he had come.

"Remember that project I mentioned?" I asked.

He canted his head and agreed.

"Is your tontine annuity project still viable?"

"I've changed the name and re-registered, but yes. It's ready to go."

I reached in my coat pocket and extracted a small paper, then placed it on the table before him. "The list of names. Do your worst. And if any of your victims pushes back, tell them you have incriminating proof of their use of illegal tech that you will not hesitate to share with the news media."

"But I—"

I held up my hand to stop him. "We do have it. It's secure and we will back you."

The paper vanished up his sleeve. He got up to leave without another word.

"Ranjit." I said.

He looked back.

"I want my damned money back."

| 13 |

Chapter Thirteen

It was nearing solstice. The last of the late fall snow had melted, revealing stark woods and barren fields. Yet calm happiness filled my heart as we turned off to Rebecca and Allan Tattie's family farm. The four of us had rented a car and we crunched and bumped along the rutted lane, lined with old maples and rusty wire fences. The majestic Victorian farmhouse was of traditional red brick, two stories, with peaked windows on the upper floor and a large bay window on the lower. It looked in good repair considering its age. Most in this area had been replaced by modern homes and spoke of practicality not style.

Nora pointed to the wooden barn and said she hoped it had some animals in it. It was a nice fantasy but unlikely since raising animals for food had been severely curtailed after the bad times. Tattie was outside, appearing as a moving mound of clothing bringing an armful of firewood for splitting. I never imagined he would be capable of manual labour like that. It made me smile.

Darwina went immediately to Rebecca. They embraced

and started a chatter which excluded the rest of us. They obviously had missed each other in the days since we had parted after our issue had been settled. Darwina had stayed behind to help Nora finish weatherproofing her home. They had reported only yesterday that it was once more fully liveable. I was happy for them. Life was good, made better by gratitude for having survived.

I stayed behind with Tattie to chop wood, but having never done it, Tattie insisted on providing an impromptu course on safety and technique which was even more appreciated once I tried it. Tattie laughed watching my first efforts and said I reminded him of the old saying that wood heats twice, first on the cutting and second in the fireplace. And I agreed with him that a heated coat was the wrong apparel for such work.

We worked together, taking turns cutting and carrying till we had enough for the night. Anticipating our thirst and appetite, Rebecca hollered out the door that she had hot apple cider and fresh baked tarts when we were ready. I took a deep breath of clean country air. My arms and back would hurt in the morning, but I did not care. This was a lovely change.

Nora and Neep had found their perfect spot close to the woodstove in the parlour. She smiled at me and pointed to the plush velour chair beside her. The wood floor creaked at almost every step. No security needed beyond that, I chuckled to myself. The walls were another matter, covered in green jungle wallpaper that made the room seem slightly foreboding. I instinctively scanned for snakes and spiders. None found, I sat beside Nora. She exhaled contentedly, Neep on her lap asleep.

"This is too warm," I complained, "and I'm all sweaty."

"Take off your sweater, then. You'll roast in that."

I did as she suggested, draping my soggy sweater over the back of the chair. "We have plenty of firewood for the night," I said, proud of our efforts.

"They have solar too, the wood for nostalgia."

"Ahh, well that deflated my ego. That was a lot of work for nostalgia."

Nora laughed. She seemed much happier lately. "Imagine we are pioneers, struggling to survive."

"They had a lot of children back then."

"Indeed, they did. And their lives were short."

"But brilliant."

We sat for a time; eyes transfixed by the flames.

Nora shifted Neep. "He's heavy."

They made a comforting picture, her wrapped in a shawl by the crackling fire, Neep, lazy eyed and loving her touch. It seemed a glimpse into a golden past, when man was connected to the essentials of life. Nora turned her head away from the fire, her face aglow. "I'm sorry I didn't let you finish back then, when I asked about why you started ReGen."

"No matter."

"You talked about feelings of incompleteness. I've thought about that a lot since then. I feel the same."

"I think most do, then we end up accepting life as it is."

"But you didn't tell me what specifically was incomplete. Your career? That's how I feel about mine, that I'm on the wrong track and may not have the time to recover."

She went on, explaining the difficulties in her work, how it had been full of promise, and now reviled and filled with suspicion, largely due to people like Kevin who had tried to subvert it. I listened, then she stopped. "Look at me, doing it again," she said. "I hate that about myself. I meant to ask about you. Was it your career which left you feeling incomplete?"

"Hmm. At the time, yes. Not now. It was so long ago. That work seems irrelevant today."

"Your wife, then?" she asked.

"We didn't have time to make a proper family. I was never able to experience it, and now it's too late. All I have are fertilized eggs in storage and fading memories."

"Fertilized eggs?"

"Yes, that's the main reason I stuck with ReGen so long."

"I understand."

I looked in her eyes and imagined her heart filled with empathy for me. But is suspected it was something else. "Could Tony not come this week?"

Nora shook her head. "There is no Tony in my life anymore."

"No?"

"Not after what he did to me...to us."

"I'm sorry," I offered, not quite meaning it.

"It's for the best. We were too much alike...careerists to the core," the bitterness colouring her laugh.

I was not sure what to say. Thankfully, our awkward moment was rescued by Rebecca who announced that supper would be served in the dining room and perhaps we would like to freshen up. Basins and towels were in each bedroom.

***

The smell drew us back like hungry dogs to the dining room, where we found a cornucopia of edible decorations arranged on the old maple dining table under a warm-light chandelier. Rebecca had outdone herself, including named place settings for each and her finest china a silver. It was nothing but spectacular. Tattie bid us be seated. He was be at the head of the table and Darwina at the other end. I was beside Nora in the middle, with little Neep relegated to a pillow under her feet. Tattie's new girlfriend was there too. She was directly across the table. I had forgotten her name and was in that awkward situation of trying to figure it out without having to ask her.

Rebecca told Tattie she was ready and took her place beside Darwina. Some Christian prayers of thanks were shared. It was sweet, all of us together like that. The room was warm and loving as were my friends. Nora and I shared a smile. I knew we would never be more than friends, but she was becoming a good one, and I would treasure that. I hoped she felt the same.

The first course was home-made vegetable soup in a special broth made from scratch, Rebecca had told us proudly. It was delicious, made with real spices which are almost impossible to find nowadays. I could have walked away satisfied after that soup, but she brought on course after course, including a real turkey, slow roasted in her wood-fired oven. We were beyond sated. Throughout it all we chatted amiably, Rebecca telling us of the native woman she had hired to harvest the wild turkey from her farm. They had become good friends with a shared interest in weaving using natural fibers. I listened to Rebecca's soothing voice and the others contributing from a place of kindness. Even Darwina seemed relaxed, and joyful even. It was lovely to connect soul-to-soul without need nor reason. This is what heaven should be, or better yet, heaven on earth.

I eventually discovered that Tattie's girlfriend was Geetika. She turned out to be pleasant and knowledgeable, and by supper's end we were sharing awful puns to the dismay of our tablemates. But it did not take long before everyone joined in, all but Tattie, who while grinning like an idiot, could not manage to remember any jokes to add to the silliness.

The laughter subsided. We were becoming sleepy, evidenced in our happy eyes and contented slouches. Then Darwina stood and clinked her crystal glass with a spoon. "I have something to announce," she said then looked to Rebecca.

I smiled, thinking I knew what was to come. They would be a couple. I was well-pleased. They would be happy, as much as life allows, at any rate.

Darwina's eyes went to each of us in turn. She took a sip of water then said, "Everyone knows that Rebecca and I are together. We love each other." We started to clap, but Darwina said, "Wait!" then laughed. "There is more. We want to have a baby!"

There was no clapping this time, just surprise. "Yeah! I will be an uncle," Tattie said appearing shocked.

It was Nora as usual who found a logical way forward. "How will you manage this? Do you have permission?"

"Yes, received it yesterday. We must take a course soon," Darwina said.

"I will carry it, of course. But we need to find a good sperm donor. The clinic will arrange the rest," Rebecca explained.

"Or do it naturally," Darwina said. "I'm not against that."

Rebecca smiled up at her. Nora elbowed me in the ribs. When I looked at her, she nodded in Rebecca's direction. I did not understand.

Nora sighed then said to everyone, "There might be another option."

I hardly had to do anything but nod my head in agreement. Over dessert, Rebecca agreed to carry my wife's fertilized eggs. Darwina wholeheartedly approved. I was in tears. I could not believe it. We rose from the table as one and shared hugs and words of love. Nora was last to embrace me. She whispered, "Are you complete now, my Amir?"

"I think so, yes. And you?"

"I have a home and our wonderful...family, and you as a friend. My career sucks, but I'll work on that next," she said laughing in my ear.

***

It had been an emotional evening, one to be engraved in memory for all-time. I hardly slept, thinking on the possibilities. This time it was not just my body that had been regenerated but my whole life. I was happy and appreciative of my friends and all they had done for me.

Rebecca was humming as she made a large pot of oatmeal. And Darwina was telling Nora that she had a lead on a home restoration project on our street, a few doors down. And restoration could be a profitable business for them both, with Nora doing the selling and planning and Darwina the hands-on. Surprisingly, Nora agreed then said, "Why don't you practise by making a baby room? You two can move in with me for the duration. Amir may like a break as well."

"It will cost—" Darwina was about to say.

"I have plenty, and those rooms need a refresh," Nora countered.

I cut in. "Speaking of profit, I have an announcement."

Nora blinked. Rebecca turned her head to hear. Darwina knew what was to come and smiled.

"I got my savings back from that annuity scam. I have plenty of credits now and wish to use them to help support the baby."

A flurry of questions ensued, answered with brevity and laughter.

"I cannot believe you did that, Amir," Nora said, the surprise flushing her face.

"Nor I," I replied, "but we can't let every outrage go unchallenged, can we? Surely, there needs to be some justice amid the harmony, if only the rough kind. And the church leaders got off lightly. They only lost some credits. No one was harmed."

Nora agreed, "Because the government chose harmony over justice. It may have been best for society, but not us. It all seemed so unfair, considering what we've been through."

"The porridge is ready. Please serve yourself," Rebecca announced. "There is cow's milk in the pitcher and maple syrup in that jug."

I was closest to the stove and first to fill my dish. It was steaming hot. I had not had porridge in years and remember hating it. But of course, I would not tell Rebecca who believed it a cure for all that ails mankind. "My Scottish ancestors lived on this and look how strong they were," she had told us while pouring oats in the boiling water.

The addition of maple syrup helped a lot. We ate contentedly, replenishing bodily needs, comforted by each other's company.

"People don't realize how much it costs to support a farm. We make almost nothing from it, and it's a constant battle to keep it as is. Good thing Allan makes a good living. I know it's a lot of pressure on him."

"I'm sure," I said. "Its much the same for those of us on Re-Gen."

"Your offer to help support the baby," Rebecca continued. "Are you sure you can afford it?"

"Yes, I'm fine."

Rebecca peered over at Darwina who had remained silent. She mouthed, "OK?"

Darwina nodded. Rebecca grinned and clapped her hands, "We'll gladly accept! Thank you, Amir."

***

And so, it came together. We made a family, legally and emotionally, to have and raise a child, my child, our child. Someone once said that it takes a village to raise one. In our case, a street of friends.

Spring came slowly that year, but not the news of Rebecca's pregnancy. She was healthy and overjoyed. We had our first foetus party that included the grand opening of the nursery built by Darwina in Nora's house. It was all in pinks and blues with animated cartoon animals on the walls and a hand-made crib crafted of wood scraps and some of Rebecca's quilts. Tattie and Geetika had a grand time helping with the shopping too.

We met Darwina's parents at the foetus party. An overly earnest couple of professional biologists who spent too much time telling everyone it was perfectly acceptable from an evolutionary perspective for lesbians to have children. Darwina rolled her eyes and whispered to me, "Now do you understand why I left home?" Despite legacy parenting issues, Darwina was doing well, her anger effectively channeled into more productive projects. She had finished renovating Nora's home and they were using it as a demo for potential customers. They had taken the plunge with their reno business, and by all accounts already had a backlog of jobs. And even little Neep had joined in, offering enhanced security systems for the renos.

We even invited Ranjit and Lei to the foetus party. They arrived arm-in-arm, shockingly tasteless draped in gaudy silks and feathers. Ranjit told me on the side that Lei was back on full ReGen and that they were building a fabulous new home in Divine Life. I was happy for them, sort of, the shame of what I had done slightly cleansed from my scared soul.

Others made an appearance too. Special Agent Rossi in a hasty meet and dash, left an enormous digital credit for Nora, Darwina and the baby, and a tearful apology which seemed sincere. Imam Zia came late, as we were cleaning up. He brought Halal gifts for mother and foetus, selected by his thoughtful wife, he said, before telling me that the church leaders had returned the library archives to the authorities, who were planning a new building for them on the site of the old library, and as a shrine to truth, openness and harmony. "So, you see, no harm done. Don't feel bad, Amir. It all turned out for the best."

I smiled at him, resisting the urge to slap the self-satisfied grin off his face.

As for me, a long life had filled me to the brim, including the empty spaces which had tormented me for so long. I had enough and knew it. I would do my best to help raise our child, but it was time to let others have their chance. That is why I booked the appointments. The first to see about changing my Will. Everything would go to Darwina, Rebecca and my unborn. The next was to see Doctor Tattie about transferring my ReGen contract to Nora. I longed to experience growing old and playing the role that nature intended. And she did not.

My home was quiet for the first time in months. I had taken the photo from its hiding place in the dining room buffet and was studying it by the spring morning light. It was a selfie we took on our honeymoon in Algonquin Park.

"I hope I did right," I said to her. "Our baby may live." I looked at her face expressing delighted approval, of me, of our new life. I kissed the picture and put it back in its folder. "I wish us together. My heart aches, I miss you so. But I must stay awhile longer. Our child may need me. Please forgive me." Something caught my eye. I rose to see. It was a robin in my backyard, the season's first.

~The End~

Albert Marsolais is a retired scientist and businessman who worked in the field of genetics and biotechnology. He lives in Ontario, Canada with his wife Laurel.